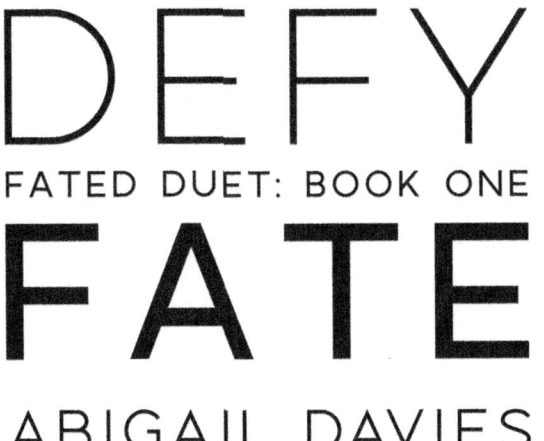

DEFY

FATED DUET: BOOK ONE

FATE

ABIGAIL DAVIES

Editing: Jennifer Roberts-Hall
Proofreading: Judy's Proofreading
Photo Credit: © Regina Wamba
Cover Design: Pink Elephant Designs
Formatting: Pink Elephant Designs

To those who suffer in silence.
Know that you are never alone.

Chapter One

ARIA

The breeze trickled through the crack in the window as we drove past all the houses in the neighborhood. It was a place where I spent a lot of my time, but it wasn't where I lived. My neighborhood was a twenty-minute drive away from this one, and definitely not as welcoming. Our apartment block was full of not-so-nice people, but it had been home for as long as I could remember.

Not much had changed in our apartment over the last seventeen years, apart from my bedroom— what had once been lilac walls with mermaid stickers was now gray, minus the stickers. There wasn't much difference between the two colors, but it was enough to show it was no longer a little girl's room. I'd gone through a phase when I was twelve and had wanted to paint it a deep red to match my hair, but Mom had put her foot down. *Thank god for that.*

"You excited?" Mom asked, her voice cutting through the pop song playing on the radio.

I blinked and turned in my seat to look at her. Her hands were gripping the steering wheel at ten and two, her short nails bare thanks to her job at the diner, and her hair was perfectly straight, not a flyaway in sight. I envied the way she could get that sleek, shiny look. My hair may have been the same deep red as hers, but it was a complete frizz ball, and nothing I ever did made it as smooth as hers.

"Yeah," I replied, my voice small.

Our hair was the only similarity between my mom and me. We were complete opposites in every other way, but I had a feeling it was why we worked so well. Where she was the life of the party, I was awkward and antisocial. Where she hated being alone, I thrived on having no one around me.

"Senior year is upon us, hunnybun"—she raised her brow and flicked her gaze to meet mine—"and you'll be leaving for college before I know it."

I shuffled in my seat and stared out of the windshield as I gripped my hands in my lap. I was equal parts excited and anxious about what would happen at the end of the school year, but I didn't want to tell Mom that. She wanted me to go off and be whatever I wanted to be, though *I* had no idea what that actually was. I read somewhere that you were most happiest when you loved what you did, but when I really thought about all the things I loved, not one of them could be a realistic career.

Running had been one of my saviors over the years, but I wasn't good enough to compete. Mom had been talking about scholarships nonstop, but I wasn't sure I wanted to apply for any of them. Running was mine—just for me. Something I did to calm my whirring thoughts. Too bad it only worked half of the time.

The silence drifted between us, and I couldn't help but wonder if this year would be any different from last year. I'd be a senior, but that didn't mean I'd become the popular girl or the girl people acknowledged while walking down the halls.

I pushed my shoulders back and sat up straighter as we pulled into the school parking lot. Only a couple of cars lingered, and I had a feeling it was all staff. At eight in the morning, the day before the school year was due to start, everyone was probably still asleep. Unlucky for me, Mom wanted to come with me to pick up my schedule, which meant we had to go before her shift at the diner.

The car shuddered to a stop, and I cringed as the loud engine cut out. It didn't bother Mom one bit, though. She simply smiled at me and hooked her thumb over her shoulder as she asked, "Ready?"

I wasn't ready. Not at all. But I nodded anyway.

I'd learned over the years that, unless you were in the mood for an epic showdown, you shouldn't disagree with my mom. She'd go to bat for you even when you didn't think she should, but that was one of the things I loved most about her.

We both got out of the car, and she slung her arm over my shoulders to pull me closer. Her five-feet-nine height compared to my five feet three was just another thing which set us apart.

A lump built in my throat as we walked through the lot, the gravel crunching underneath Mom's Converse and my ballet flats. The ten steps to the light-blue double doors loomed closer, and if I hesitated, Mom didn't mention it.

School used to be my safe haven—a place where I could immerse myself in everything possible. But the older I got, the more I dreaded coming here. Middle school was bad, but high school was plain terror. I'd learned coping techniques over the years, one of which was to try and go by unnoticed. I kept my gaze fixated to the floor, only looking up when absolutely necessary. I didn't initiate conversation with anyone, and most importantly, I never answered students back when they called me names. It worked…most of the time.

Even though the hallway lined with gray lockers was empty, that same pit in the bottom of my stomach, the one that always appeared when I was on school grounds, was evident. My palms started to sweat, and my body screamed to pull away from my mom and turn back around, but I wasn't a quitter.

One year.

I only had one year left in this place, and then I'd be gone forever.

My mind was a whirl as we entered the main office and greeted the office secretary, Mrs. Madden. Her gray hair and worn face already showed signs of tiredness, and the school year hadn't officially begun yet. Mrs. Madden handed me my schedule and reeled off my new locker number. Mom was adamant we find my new locker in the senior hall, walking ahead and calling out the numbers scribed on each one as she went. We'd done this every year since I'd started here, and today wouldn't be any different.

"Here!" she announced, holding her arms wide.

I smiled and gazed around. Between two class-rooms stood a row of ten lockers, and mine was right in the middle. I hated being in the middle, but I prayed Hope's locker would be nearby.

Hope. The one person who attended school and did exactly what her name said—gave me hope.

"Can we go now?" I asked Mom, hoping I didn't sound too whiney. I didn't want to be here any longer than I already had to be. I wanted to be back in my bedroom with my pile of throw pillows I kept on my bed—technically, they weren't throw pillows because I never actually threw them off the bed when I slept—and lose myself in a book.

Mom's smile dropped at the corners, but she soon built it back up and flashed it full force as she stepped toward me. "Of course." She swung her arm around mine as we walked past the classroom door and down the hall.

The senior hallway was the one farthest back in the school, so we had to walk back past the office to get out—an office where students were starting to arrive. The sight of letterman jackets had my gaze veering to the floor and my hand lifting to push some hair over my face. The last thing I needed was for any of the football players to notice me, especially with Mom standing next to me. I didn't understand why, in this technological savage age, they couldn't just email our schedule to us?

Within minutes, we were back in the car and heading toward the diner. The diner sat almost exactly between school and our apartment. I wasn't sure how my mom had gotten me into the school back when I'd been a freshman because it was technically out of our district, but she'd managed it anyway. Maybe she'd used the diner address? I could still hear the echo of her words in my head the summer before freshman year: "Only the best for you, hunnybun." She always said that, no matter what we were doing. Everything she did was to make my life better. Maybe she thought if she did that then I wouldn't remember what happened nine years ago, and that the memories would magically disappear? Whatever the case, she was wrong. Nothing would stop me from thinking about the night that changed everything. Nothing could erase the images in my head.

I glanced over at her and grinned as she tried her best to dance and drive at the same time. She was having a great time, while I was over here dreading the next year of my life. I couldn't show her that, though. If she were going to put on a brave face, then I'd do exactly the same. Every day of my high school life was about going by unnoticed, and I knew running track would destroy that, but maybe it was time for a change. Maybe it was time I pushed out of my comfort zone, even if it was only to try out.

"Mom?" She pulled into a space in the diner lot and hummed in response. "I think I'll try out for track this year."

Her eyes widened, and her head swiveled to face me. "I…you…" Mom was never lost for words. I chuckled and unclipped my belt while she got herself together. "You are?"

I shrugged. For years she'd been trying to get me to try out for the track team. "It's my senior year. I may as well try, right?"

"Yes!" She practically threw herself over the center console and wrapped her arms around me.

"This is going to be the best year. I can feel it in my bones, Aria." She pulled back and grasped each side of my face. "Do you feel it?"

I didn't, but I nodded anyway. *Fake it until you make it, right?*

———

ARIA

Sleep hadn't come easy, no matter what I tried: A soothing bath before I threw myself into my throw pillows, lavender mist to help ease my body into relaxation, counting sheep. None of it helped me get to sleep until three this morning. And now it was four hours later, and I resembled a zombie.

I pushed myself out of bed, brushed my teeth, and sorted my face out with minimal makeup before trying to tame my hair into submission. The end look was a beach wave, but I kind of dug it. It was better than the frizz ball it had been. I'd laid my clothes out last night—skinny black jeans, a white T-shirt with a rainbow on the front, and my trusty combat boots—so after one final check in the mirror, I declared myself ready.

"Aria?" a deep voice called from the other side of my bedroom door followed by a knock. "I made you breakfast."

A grin spread over my face as I picked up my

backpack and leather jacket that I probably wouldn't need thanks to the never-ending summer, but the last time I'd left it at home, I got caught in the rain. I pulled open the door and tilted my head to the side as I took in one of the men who had come into my life and made me trust again. He didn't understand why it took five years of dating my mom for me to talk to him properly, but Sal was a patient man. He didn't push and knew when to back off, but most importantly, he was always there, no matter what.

"You did?" I asked him, trying to push my grin down a notch, but it wasn't working. I couldn't remember the last time someone had made me breakfast on my first day of school. Mom was always so busy with work that we usually grabbed something on the go.

Sal swiped his hand down his face and over the scruff shadowing his jaw, trying his hardest to come off as casual, but he was failing majorly. "I was cooking anyway."

I stepped out of my room and raised a brow. "So you *cooked* me breakfast?"

Sal's nostrils flared, but I'd learned a long time ago this happened for one of two reasons: he was angry or embarrassed. Today, I was going with the latter. "Get your ass in the kitchen and eat before your mom wakes up and starts harassing you." His words were a complete contrast to his tone, but he didn't have to tell me twice. The threat of Mom talking nonstop before my first day back at the hell-hole people liked to call school was enough to get my butt moving.

The short hallway that housed our bedrooms and compact bathroom led into the living room and kitchen separated only by a break between carpet and tiles. The scent of bacon permeated the air, and I was really hoping there'd be a couple of pancakes thrown in there too, and maybe some hash browns just for fun.

Sal didn't disappoint, because as soon as I sat my ass in one of the two chairs at the dining table, I was greeted with exactly that. But there was only one plate: mine.

"You were already cooking, huh?" I asked, making a show of glancing around at the absence of any other food.

Sal lifted his mug filled with black coffee to his lips and grunted. "That's what I said, didn't I?"

I shook my head and placed a strip of crispy bacon in my mouth. I may have been nervous and dreading walking back into those halls, but that didn't mean my body would reject the delicious food. It would probably be the only meal I'd eat sitting at a table today because as soon as lunchtime rolled around, I'd head straight for my safe place: under the bleachers.

With only half a pancake left on my plate, footsteps sounded down the hallway, and I heard a groan that could only be deciphered as, "Coffee."

Mom drifted into the kitchen—drifted was a nice word. She practically dragged herself. She gratefully took the cup Sal handed her and groaned again as she took the first sip. By the time I'd finished the last of my breakfast, she'd drunk half of her coffee and resembled more of a human.

"Morning," she announced, first looking at me and then Sal.

"Morning," I answered back.

"Jan," Sal said with a nod. I nearly snorted at his greeting, which I should have been used to by now. You'd think he would at least have said good morning or maybe greeted her with a kiss, but that wasn't Sal's way. He was who he was, and that was the reason my mom loved him so much.

Mom blinked several times, and then she darted over to me. "It's your first day back, and I overslept!"

"No biggie." I shrugged, pushed myself up out of the chair, and carried my plate over to the sink.

"I'll do that," Mom said, following me over and ripping the plate out of my hand. "Give me ten minutes, and I'll be ready to take you."

I glanced at the clock on the wall and shook my head. "I need to leave now."

"Crap!" The plate clanged in the sink as she scurried across the kitchen, and I winced. "I—"

"I'll take her." We both swung our attention over to Sal who stood in the same spot but with keys dangling from his fingers.

"I can't miss her last first day of school," Mom whispered. "I'm coming with you."

"Mom." I blinked and blinked again. She was wearing an old band T-shirt and booty shorts. "Not like that."

"I won't get out of the car." She grabbed my hand and walked past the table where she managed to hook my bag and jacket over her other arm without even letting me go. "Come on, Hope is probably waiting for you."

Crap. She was right. We'd arranged to meet on the south side of the lot, and she was probably already there.

I didn't bother trying to get Mom to lessen her grip on my arm as we exited the apartment because it would be a useless task. We all piled into Sal's pickup truck and off we went with Mom squished in the middle but bouncing in her seat. I wasn't sure what she was saying on the way, because the entire fifteen-minute drive I was trying not to throw up what I'd eaten. Maybe a big breakfast the first day of school wasn't such a good idea after all.

"Do you have everything?" Mom asked, and from the look on her face, it was definitely not the first time she'd asked me.

"I—"

"Cell, backpack, notepads, pens——"

"Yeah, I got everything," I interrupted, knowing she'd go into everything I should always have on me, including sanitary products, body spray, and a rape whistle. Mom made sure I was prepared no matter what. I loved her for it, but she was overkill sometimes. I had to make allowances, though. We'd gone through hell together, even though she liked to pretend it never happened.

Sal pulled into the school lot, and I slapped my palm against his dash. "There's Hope." He slammed on his brakes, not giving one crap that he was now blocking the entrance.

"We're both working the late shift, but call me if you need me!" Mom shouted as I pushed out of the truck.

"Have a good day," Sal said in his usual gruff tone.

I nodded as my feet hit the gravel. "Okay." I turned around. "I'll probably go see how Belle's first day was after school."

Mom grinned. "I had a feeling you might. See you tomorrow morning, hunnybun."

I rolled my eyes at her nickname and slammed the door shut. My gaze was set on Hope as she tried to make herself one with the wall. She didn't want to draw attention to her ink-black hair and pale face. She wasn't a goth, but she naturally looked like one. I thought she resembled more of a grunge

Snow White, but she was adamant she was more Wednesday Addams.

The lot was filling with cars now that Sal and Mom had pulled out, and by the time I got to Hope, the loudness sounded more like a party—not that I had ever been invited to a high school party.

"And so it begins," Hope said, not looking at me but staring at something in the lot.

I tried to see what she was looking at, but I didn't have to wait long. The football players were surrounded by cheerleaders, all in their uniforms to start the year off with a bang. Football season would take over everything for the next few months.

"I have a feeling this year will be different," I murmured, trying to believe the words as they came out of my mouth.

Hope raised her brows and stared at me like I'd lost my mind. And maybe I had. "Jesus, Aria. Is that why you wore your rainbow T-shirt?"

I shrugged. "Gotta think positive, right?"

She snorted and pushed off the wall. "Let's see how long that lasts."

We walked side by side, trying to be as invisible as possible, but as soon as we neared the footballers and cheerleaders, we realized it wasn't going to happen.

"Hey, look! It's Ghost and Carrot leading the way through the darkness."

I wasn't sure which one of them said it, but I

had an inkling it was Harry—named after the Prince of England. He didn't have ginger hair, but I was sure he was working an early serving bald patch. Served him right for being such a huge douche.

"Forty-nine seconds," I announced to Hope as we walked up the steps and through the double doors. "It lasted forty-nine seconds."

"New record?" she asked, gripping her backpack like it was a shield against all the looks burning our backs.

"Yep."

We made it into the senior hall and to our lockers—just our luck, our lockers were on opposite ends. I wasn't sure how they worked out who went where, but if it were alphabetical, that would mean…

"Great, I'm next to her," a bitchy voice said.

I closed my eyes, took a breath, and gripped the lock in my hand. It was only a combination of three numbers, but I couldn't for the life of me remember what they were, not with Jasmine standing next to me.

"Jasmine," I greeted, my voice cracking halfway through the one word. I glanced at her, taking in the perfectly curled blond hair and face of impeccable makeup. She didn't even look like a high school senior. More like a twenty-five-year-old woman who was going out for the night.

Jasmine lifted her lip into a sneer and stepped toward her locker, shoulder barging me at the same time. A few echoes of laughter followed her move, causing my cheeks to burn. It looked more like a sunburn than an actual blush—another downside to having my hair color.

My fingers slid from around the unopened lock. I didn't even need to put anything in there, not yet anyway. Hope's black hair stood out in the crowd as she made her way back to me, and I decided to forgo the locker and head straight to class instead.

I ignored the comments from Jasmine's little cheerleading minions as I stepped past them and walked toward Hope. "I don't know why we always end up so far apart," Hope whined when we met in the middle of the hallway. We both shuffled off to the side, knowing we now had to go in opposite directions. We'd studied each other's schedules last night, and the only class we had together was PE on Friday afternoons—a subject Hope hated with a passion.

"Because the world is out to get us," I said sarcastically, but part of me wondered why fate had chosen to throw the things at me that it had. Why couldn't I have been one of the popular girls? It was day one of the school year, and I already wanted to go home and get back into my nice, comfy bed.

Hope nodded, agreeing with me, and then laughed. "Ugh. I hate school."

"Feeling's mutual." I gazed around the senior hall, taking in all the greetings between friends who hadn't seen each other over summer. I was glad Hope and I had managed to at least spend a few days together, plus our constant text messages.

"Meet you at lunch?" she asked, already stepping away from me to head to her first class.

"Yep. Bleachers?"

"You got it."

We both nodded at each other, a silent, "good luck" of sorts, and headed off. My first class was AP English and went by like a breeze, along with chemistry, my second class. My third classroom was next to my locker, and I finally had salvation from the heavy books from my first two classes. At least this time, Jasmine was nowhere to be seen as I opened up my locker and stacked the books onto the top shelf.

The hallway was nearly empty by the time I managed to click the lock on my locker. Harry—the football player—was the first person I saw when I entered the classroom, and if his smirk was anything to go by, he'd spotted me too.

The layout of the room was pretty standard: five rows with five desks, jocks at the back, nerds at the front. There were only two seats left, and luckily for me, one of them was in a perfect position. I always headed for a middle-of-the-row seat: far enough away from the people in the back but not too close to the front—the invisible seats.

I settled into the third seat back on the second row in, closer to the teacher's desk than I liked, but it was either this or be one desk in front of Harry.

The teacher wasn't here yet which meant most of the students were being as loud as they could be, but as I dipped down to pull my notebook and pen out of my bag, it quieted to an eerie silence. There had been murmurings of a new teacher during my last class, but no one had mentioned their name. I just hoped it wasn't—

"Good morning, students."

My eyes widened, and my breath stuttered in my chest. *That voice.* It was a voice I would never forget, not since the first time I heard it when I was eight years old. The timbre was deeper than it had been back then, but the tone was the exact same.

It couldn't be.

How could he be here? In my world history class of all places. No one had told me he was back.

"I'll check attendance, and then we'll go over the schedule for this semester."

My lungs struggled to pull in air, but as soon as I looked to the front of the class, it whooshed out of me. My first ever crush stood front and center. A crush I had been sure was love when I was a little girl. I knew the difference now, but that didn't stop my body's reaction.

I tried to halt the memories flashing through my brain, but the first time he'd touched me was on repeat. I'd known him six months before the worst night of my life happened, but it had been the first time he'd held me and promised to make it all better. He'd had a true glimpse of what my life had been like up to that point, but he didn't really know.

None of them truly knew.

Chapter Two

CADE

I hadn't always wanted to be a teacher.

When I was a teenager, I was sure I would be a professional athlete. I probably could have if I had wanted it bad enough—if I'd have applied myself and worked toward one goal. But I hadn't. I hadn't wanted anything enough to go in one clear direction. I'd been floating through each day, angry at the world and what it had served me with. But the day I coached some kids while in my freshman year of college, I knew what I was meant to do.

Community outreach had been a requirement of being part of the lacrosse college team, and it was there I realized I wanted to coach kids. I wanted to be a driving force to the kids who had a dream of being an athlete—show them they could be that even if they thought they couldn't. I wanted to help them become exactly who they wanted to be.

Becoming a teacher was simply a perk of being a coach because it meant I got the best of both worlds. A couple of classes a day in a shirt, tie, and slacks, and then I could spend the rest of my time in sweats, teaching PE and coaching the next generation of athletes.

I'd built up contacts over my four years at college, and my plan had always been to stay there instead of moving back home. But my senior year, everything changed in the blink of an eye. One tragic event changed the course of my entire life. I'd tried to create a life for myself—tried to push everything out of my mind—but it hadn't worked. Being constantly reminded of it every day wasn't good for anyone.

For three years, I'd tried my hardest to put it all behind me, but as soon as my stepmom, Lola, told me about a vacancy so close to home, I knew fate had stepped in to take me down a different path. I'd moved back home a week ago, and now I was ready to start fresh. I also got to spend more time with my little sister, Belle—PB as I liked to call her—and my little brother, Asher. My family was everything to me.

More so now than ever…

My introduction to teaching in the same school

I'd attended as a student had come in the form of freshmen, but now I was in the big leagues. Senior class. One year until these kids would be off to college or looking for employment. I moved over to the desk and pulled out my laptop, feeling several sets of eyes burning through the side of my face. My lips wanted to curve up into a grin, but I held them down, remembering what it was like when a new teacher would start at school. Especially if that teacher was under the age of thirty.

"I'll call your name out, and I want you to raise your hand and tell me a fact about yourself." I glanced up, not really taking in any of the faces, and then concentrated back on my screen. It felt a little like elementary school when teachers would call out students' names every morning, but this would be a good icebreaker.

"Lydia."

"Here," a soft voice announced. She was in the front row, her hair pulled back into a tight ponytail, and glasses too big for her face. "I love math."

I nodded and smiled. "Nice to meet you, Lydia."

I went through the list, frowning when I got halfway. "Aria…" I blinked, sure I read it wrong. "Aria Sayer?" My voice was shaky, a little unsure of whether I'd said the words right, but I looked up anyway, expecting to see the little girl I used to know. There was no way she was a senior already…

"Here." My head snapped up at the tone that couldn't be mistaken for anyone but the eight-year-old girl who had tried to nurse me back to health when I was sixteen. A girl who had sat by my side while her mom made us grilled cheese. A girl who now looked…like a woman.

I couldn't take my eyes off Aria. I couldn't stop staring at her wavy red hair and the small button nose I knew would be covered with the splattering of freckles.

Damn. I couldn't even remember the last time I'd seen her. Maybe five years ago? No, four years…

Had she really changed that much?

"I…I like to run."

I raised a brow, surprised by her answer. I hadn't been expecting it to come out of her mouth, but that was exactly who Aria was—unexpected. At least, the Aria I remembered.

I kept my gaze locked with hers for an extra second, trying to convey something I wasn't sure of, and then moved on to the rest of the students. I wasn't sure whether she'd want people to know that we knew each other, so I'd keep my mouth closed for now and teach the class in the same way I did any other time. By the time I'd gone through everyone's names, and given them the rundown of what we'd be learning over the next semester, we only had five minutes left.

"You can leave early for lunch," I told them with

a quick look at my watch. We weren't meant to let classes out early, but these were seniors, most of them about to turn eighteen, so they could be trusted—I hoped.

Cheers rang out, and I shook my head with a grin. It was hard getting used to the fact I was the teacher and not the student. I had a feeling I'd never quite get used to it. Inside, I'd always be the sixteen-year-old kid who loved lacrosse and any kind of competitive sport.

Students filed out of the room as I closed my laptop and slid it into my bag, but I was hyperaware of Aria taking her time to leave the class. When I looked up, she was standing in the aisle, looking down at her hands and gnawing on her bottom lip.

"Aria?" I called.

"Cade—I mean…" She cleared her throat and stepped toward me, her gaze landing on mine. "Mr. Easton." She shook her head and wrinkled up her nose. "That's so freaking weird."

I crossed my arms over my chest. "It is when you're saying it. Sounds like you're talking about my dad."

She snorted and gripped the edges of her leather jacket, causing me to flick my gaze down to her T-shirt and the rainbow painted onto it. "Uncle Brody would kill me if I called him that."

My lips quirked on one side. My dad wasn't really her uncle, but she'd taken to calling him that when she was ten and had to stay the night after Jan had broken her arm at the diner. Pretty sure that was the night Sal had finally told Jan how he felt about her.

Things changed so fast, and I wondered how many things were now different. It wasn't that I hadn't visited, because I had. It was just…different because I hadn't seen her.

"How's your mom?" I asked, trying to make small talk. I'd seen her mom on my last visit home, but that had been six months ago. The way her eyes stared at mine was the same as always—like she saw right through me.

The bell rang out for lunch, but neither of us moved. "She's good. Sal is practically living with us now." She glanced away, staring out the wall of windows that looked out onto the field and track. "No one told me you were back."

I shrugged even though she couldn't see it. "I didn't know myself until a couple days back."

She nodded but didn't say anything else. She was always good at that: internalizing everything she was thinking. Aria never said anything unless she meant it. She had always been an overthinker, whereas I spoke first and asked questions later, and the way she was talking and acting meant that hadn't changed.

There was a time I knew her better than anyone. Knew when she was sad and what she was sad about. Knew when she needed distracting or when she just wanted to talk. Most people wouldn't have thought it normal for a sixteen-year-old to be so close to an eight-year-old, but they hadn't been through what we had. They didn't understand the darkness that surrounded our history.

But I'd dropped her as soon as I started college. I'd forgotten all about Aria and what she'd been through, and I was only now realizing what a shit thing that was to do.

"There you are!" I whipped my head toward the open door and frowned at the dark-haired girl. "Come on, Aria. We need out of these hallways—" The girl finally looked at me and stumbled back a step. "Crap. Sorry, sir, I didn't realize—"

"You're fine," I said, waving my hand and shouldering my bag. "Aria was just leaving."

Aria hesitated and then shook her head. She walked forward, stopping a couple of feet in front of me, and whispered, "I'm glad you're home."

I swallowed against the lump in my throat and croaked out, "Me too."

Neither of us looked away for a couple of seconds, and then her lips lifted into a small smile. A smile I hadn't even known I'd missed until she flashed it my way. "Don't think this gives you automatic Belle and Asher rights," she warned with a raised brow. "I still get first dibs."

She sauntered out of the room, and it wasn't

until she was turning out of the doorway that I managed to say, "They're my siblings, not yours." And I realized that I sounded like a kid again. I'd only been around her for an hour, and she was already bringing out the old Cade. The Cade who didn't have a care in the world. The Cade who flew by the seat of his pants. That Cade had disappeared and I wasn't sure whether I wanted him back or not. He was the old me, but also the me I craved to be again.

Life had a way of throwing things at you, but surely there was a time when there was too much shit flung your way? They said things happened in threes, and that night, it was the exact number of people who had died. People who had their lives cut short.

All because of me.

If I hadn't stepped in the car at that exact moment. If I hadn't forgotten my wallet and had to go back inside to get it. If I had left only ten seconds later or ten seconds earlier…

The world was full of what-ifs.

What-ifs that kept me up at night.

What-ifs that changed the way I thought.

What-ifs that had changed my life.

———

CADE

"Mom said you're staying for good," Belle said from beside me on the couch. I hadn't moved from the time I walked in the door, and she'd accosted me to watch a horse cartoon with her.

"I am," I told her, shifting to the side and turning to face the living room door as Asher screamed from upstairs. The kid was only four, but he was full of sheer determination—he knew what he wanted, and he didn't shy away from demanding it.

Belle dipped her hand into the bowl of chips on her lap and stared up at me as she brought one to her mouth and crunched slowly. Lola would kill me if she knew I'd allowed Belle to eat junk food this close to bedtime, but big brothers were allowed to bend the rules for their little sisters.

"And you're a teacher now?"

"Yep." I grabbed a chip from the bowl and raised my hands in surrender when she narrowed her eyes at me.

"You're meant to ask, Cade," Belle reprimanded, sounding more and more like the perfect mix of Lola and my dad.

"May I have a chip?"

Her screwed-up angry features relaxed back into the sweet girl she was *half of the time*. "You may." She stared back at the TV, chowing down on her chips as the horse made a jump and everyone clapped. "I hate my teacher."

"You do?" I frowned. How could she hate her teacher after only one day? And what was there to hate about someone who taught a group of eight-year-olds? It was my idea of hell but to each their own and all that.

"Yeah. Henry pulled my hair at lunch, so I told him I was going to call the cops." She threw her hands up in the air, the bowl of chips wavering precariously on her lap as she blinked at me. "Miss Ferry said I couldn't call the cops, so I told her my dad is in the PDA, and so are my uncles, and they'd arrest her for telling me what to do."

"DEA," I corrected, trying my utmost hardest to keep a straight face, but it was so hard with her serious expression. Thank god she didn't have access to a cell because I had no doubt she'd call them from her school to come and rescue her, and what was even scarier was that they'd probably do it.

"What?"

"Dad's in the DEA, not PDA. PDA means something—"

"Whatever," she cut me off and waved her arms in the air, obviously having had enough of me correcting her. "She sent me to the principal"—her eyes widened in horror—"and now I have to miss recess tomorrow." She groaned and pushed herself lower on the sofa. "School sucks."

"I'm sure it's not that bad, PB. Your teacher—"

"Ugh! You don't understand—"

The doorbell rang out, and I was literally saved by the bell. PB's face was becoming redder and redder the more she talked about her day at school, and I was hoping whoever this was would make her forget about it, or at least stop her from taking it out on me because I didn't "understand."

"I'll get it!" Belle shouted, throwing her bowl of chips off her lap and showering me with them. She made a mad dash for the door and was pulling it open before I even got the chance to stand up. "Finally! A girl who will understand!"

"Hello to you too, Belle." Aria's voice was the first thing I heard, and then I saw her smiling face. She looked different outside the classroom. More relaxed and…I couldn't put my finger on it, but she appeared to be more like the Aria I'd known. I still couldn't believe how much she'd changed. It hadn't felt like I was gone that many years, but evidently, I had.

"Hi," Belle replied as she walked back over to the sofa and threw herself down onto it.

The door clicked shut and Aria followed her in, flashing me a smaller version of the smile she'd sent Belle's way. "Hey, Cade."

"Hey," I replied, trying to get all the chips back in the bowl before Lola came downstairs from putting Asher to bed and found out what I'd supplied her only daughter with.

"Aria, you'll understand." Belle pushed up off the sofa and pointed at the seat she'd been sitting in. "Sit, let me tell you about my day."

Aria did as she was told but leaned closer to me and whispered, "I see Bossy Belle is present today." Her flowery perfume drifted toward me, and I raised a brow. That was something new, but then, the last time I'd seen her she'd been an awkward teen, and now she was so much more than that. She was practically a woman. I dipped my gaze to her chest and the rainbow on her T-shirt. She was definitely a woman.

Shit, I did not need to be looking *there*.

"Yeah, maybe I should change PB to BB?"

Aria turned to face me. "What does PB mean anyway?"

"Princess Belle," I told her. I'd given her the nickname when she was a baby, and it had stuck.

Belle cleared her throat, and we both whipped our head around to face her. She pulled in a dramatic breath and blurted out, "So Henry pulled my hair—"

"No!" Aria gasped, her sweet face changing in the blink of an eye. Gone were the delicate features. In its place was a frown and lips in a firm, straight line. "Again? That little shi—"

"Language," I coughed.

"Poobag," Aria finished, flicking her gaze to mine. Her light-brown eyes looked more like honey in this light, and I hated I noticed that. I shuffled a little away from her. We were too close, and also out of the classroom, but that didn't mean I wasn't still her teacher.

Shit, what the hell was going on with me today? It was the stress of a new day on the job, that was all. Maybe I should concentrate on eating the chips in my lap and keeping my hands occupied and my attention on Belle. Yep, that was what I would do.

"That's what I said!" Belle shouted, her hands now on her hips as she paced back and forth. "I told him I was gonna call the cops on him, but Miss Ferry"—she screwed up her face—"told me I couldn't. So I told her my dad was PDA—"

Aria didn't do as good a job as me in holding in her laughter. It burst out of her, and I couldn't remember the last time I'd seen her lose control like that, but just hearing the sound and watching the way her body lost control had me grinning like a fool. It was always the smallest things that would set her off, and she had the kind of laugh you couldn't help but join in with. It was addictive. Pure and simple.

"What?" Belle asked, clearly getting annoyed. "What did I say?"

"Well." Aria tried to get ahold of herself as she

wiped at her face. "PDA means public display of affection. I think you mean DEA?"

"Ugh. You sound like Cade." Belle swiped her hand through the air and rolled her eyes. "What I was saying is that I hate my teacher. She's bossy, and—"

"Bossy," I whispered out of the corner of my mouth, which set Aria off again.

It had been years since we'd sat on this sofa together and laughed, but it felt like only yesterday she was pacing in front of me the same way Belle was now and telling me I shouldn't move because of my bullet wound in my shoulder. If Belle was bossy now, she had nothing on Aria back then.

"You adults don't understand anything!" Belle shouted and stomped out of the room and up the stairs, leaving me wide-eyed and wondering what happened to the sweet Belle I'd last seen a couple of months ago.

"Well…" I raised my brows and turned to face Aria. "She's…"

"Bossy." Aria nodded. "She's probably tired from her first day back. Plus, that Henry is a shit bag."

"Hey now." I stood and gripped the bowl of chips in my hand as I looked down at her. "You shouldn't talk about a kid like that."

"Yeah?" She raised her own brows in response and stood. "That 'kid' has been picking on Belle for the last twelve months straight, but she won't tell anyone. She vents to me, but I'm sworn to secrecy—ah, shit." Her shoulders drooped. "I just blew our secret code contract." Aria threw her hands up in the air and narrowed her eyes on me. "You made me break my contract."

"Me?" I pointed at my chest, wondering what dimension I'd found myself in which made all the women throw their anger my way. "What did I do?"

"You...never mind." Aria spun around, leaving the room in the same way Belle had, and ran up the stairs.

I wasn't sure what the hell had happened, but I was starting to realize things were different now. I'd been gone too long to simply slot back into the life I'd left when I was eighteen. Belle was practically a moody teenager, and Aria was no longer the little girl who could be entertained by poo jokes.

Things had changed, but so had I.

I wasn't sure I'd ever be the same again, and just as the thought occurred to me, I itched to go for a run. To clear my mind of everything and concentrate on the beat of my sneakers hitting the sidewalk. I craved the burn it would cause my muscles, and before I knew it, I was changed and knocking on Belle's bedroom door.

"Aria?" I pushed the door open a crack. Aria and Belle were sitting on the bed and reading a story. "I need to head out, and Lola is putting Asher to bed. Could you watch Belle until she's finished?"

Aria blinked several times, her gaze roving from my sneakers, over my shorts, and stopping on my tank top and the tattoos I kept covered up at school.

"You run?" she asked, her voice small. I remembered what she'd said in class earlier today. She liked to run too, and I couldn't help but wonder if she'd try out for the track team in a couple of weeks.

"Only when I need to clear my head," I told her, admitting more to her than I ever had to anyone else. There was always a silent understanding between us, ever since I'd first met her. We were secret keepers—and pretty good ones at that.

But I'd never tell her why I needed to clear my head.

I wouldn't tell her how the sound of Asher screaming his refusal to have a bath brought back memories of that night. I wouldn't tell her how the sound of footsteps echoing on the stairs reminded me of the boots hitting the tarmac and heading toward the burning vehicle I'd been trapped in.

I wouldn't tell her anything, because no one would ever understand what had happened that night. No one would ever feel the pain I felt.

Aria nodded, and Belle looked over her shoulder, her tired, blue eyes piercing through me. I was here to start over, to be closer to my family, but that didn't mean I didn't have baggage.

"Sure," Aria whispered.

"Thanks." I didn't say anything else as I moved back, pushed my earbuds into my ears, and headed down the stairs and out the front door.

I'd run until all the thoughts had evaporated, and then I'd go a little longer to make sure they stayed away, if only for one night.

Chapter Three

ARIA

The first week back had gone by at a snail's pace, but it was finally Friday. Only one day left until I could spend two days to myself without anyone else around to bug me or want to talk to me. I could run for hours with my music blasting in my ears, and not one person would disturb me. It would be pure bliss. But that soon evaporated when I realized Cade would be teaching my last class of the day: PE.

The school had been abuzz with his arrival and students telling people who he was and who his dad was. People knew of Uncle Brody, but none of them *really* knew him. They had heard the rumors of him leaving his wife nearly a decade ago for someone nearly half his age, but they didn't understand who they were, or how you could feel their love for each other when you were in a room with them. They didn't understand how fate worked, and neither did I, but I understood that love didn't care about boundaries and rules because love was love, no matter how you viewed it.

"So you grew up with him?" Hope asked as we walked around the track to warm up.

"Not exactly." I'd finally given in and told Hope I knew Cade—*Mr. Easton*, I kept reminding myself. I'd nearly slipped up several times this week when I'd seen him around school. Hope had done her best impression of a blowfish when I hit her with that fact this morning.

I couldn't get the look on his face out of my mind when he'd stood in Belle's doorway. The pain shining in his eyes was obvious for everyone to see. Or maybe it was just me. Maybe I could recognize it because I felt it too.

"I met him when I was eight." I huffed out a breath, my legs begging me to go faster, but I had to keep pace with Hope, if only for a little while. "My mom worked with Lola—Brody's wife—and Sal is good friends with his dad."

"Wow." Hope blinked and halted halfway on the track, trying to catch her breath. We'd barely moved, and she was already tired. "And he was a teenager at the time?"

"Yep." I swiped my arm over my face to wipe some of the sweat away and to keep myself busy.

"He was maybe fifteen, sixteen, at the time." I shrugged and stretched my arms over my chest to get ready to take off. We had a routine we'd gained over the years. I'd do one lap at Hope's pace, and then I could take off and lose myself in the rhythm of my feet hitting the ground. "He left for college a couple of years after that, and I barely saw him."

"Wait..." Hope stepped forward, her eyes narrowing as she stared at me. "Did you have a crush on him?"

I opened my mouth, about to deny it, but she gasped, seeing the truth written all over my face. Instead of answering her, I took off, running away from her exactly like I did with everything else. I could feel the burning of my cheeks as I ran around the track, but the burn in my thighs was a welcome one. All I wanted was to lose myself—tire my muscles out the best I possibly could. This was only meant to be a warm-up, but running was never that for me. It was an escape, something that could never be taken away from me.

I was so inside my own head that I hadn't realized I was on the fourth lap when a whistle blew and Cade's booming voice shouted, "Everyone in the middle to pick teams."

Great. Team sports. Just what I loved the most.

I was a solo athlete, and the old PE teacher knew this, which was why she would let me run track for most of the class. But from the way Cade was staring at me and waving me toward him, I didn't think I'd get away with it this time.

He wasn't wearing his usual shirt and dress pants, but instead a full-sleeved training top and sweatpants. You could see every outline of muscle on his top half, and I knew, for a fact, every other girl in class noticed.

I made it to the middle of the field, huffing and puffing as I tried to regulate my breathing. Cade chose the captains: Jasmine and one of her friends. They went through every person in the senior class, leaving Hope and me until last, which meant we'd be on opposing teams.

I stood awkwardly at the edge of the team, not wanting to get involved as Cade told us the rules to lacrosse. I'd never played in my life, and I wasn't sure any of the other girls had either. We'd had a lacrosse team when I first started as a freshman, but it ended that year when our team came in last in the championship.

Sticks were handed out, but thank god only ten people were on a team because it meant another five girls and I could sit and watch.

Hope was placed in the goalie position, and I grinned at her. She stuck her tongue out in response and completely missed a goal being shot toward her. It flew by her head, and she stumbled to the side, mouthing, "What the fuck," at me. I couldn't help but laugh at her, but all too soon, Cade was telling me to get on the field.

I didn't have a problem sprinting down the pitch, but what I did have a problem with was actually catching the ball with my stick and net thing, and if I did catch it, it was knocked out of it more or less right away. This was the exact reason I only relied on my feet to do the moving because, as soon as another object was added to the mix, I lost all sense of equilibrium.

"Good job today, girls!" Cade shouted and clapped his hands. "Next week, we'll work on some techniques. Have a good weekend."

All the girls headed for the locker rooms, but Hope and I stayed back, not wanting to be in a confined space with them all. The last time we'd done that in sophomore year, we'd ended up "losing" half of our clothes and having to wear some weird lost-and-found stuff for the rest of the day. Never again.

"You girls heading in to get changed?" Cade asked as he put the sticks in the two barrels he'd had out here when we first warmed up.

Hope and I looked at each other then back to him. I may have known him as Cade, but here he was Mr. Easton, and there was no way I was going to tell him why we hung back and waited until everyone was finished.

"Do you need help packing away?" I asked instead of answering his question.

"I…" Cade frowned as he watched me and then flicked his gaze to the goals. "You can take those down if you want?"

"Sure." I didn't say another word as I walked over to the one Hope had been standing in and started to take it down. I may not have been good at the actual sport, but I could figure out any puzzle like a pro, and that was exactly what taking these goals down was. We had them bundled up in no time.

We headed over to where Cade was marking some things off a clipboard.

"Thanks, girls." Cade grinned, the kind of grin he used to flash at me, and I blinked. There'd been a time where I skipped into his house and waited for that grin to come my way, but that was before…

Before that day.

Before my life changed forever.

I'd never again be that girl, the one he first met, and the single thought sobered me and had me pulling back my shoulders. I had to remember where I was, but most importantly, *who* I was. I wasn't like most of the girls at this school. Their idea of baggage was their parents not buying them the car they wanted. Or not getting to go away to Mexico for their eighteenth birthday.

"No problem," I answered Cade, my tone

coming out stiff and not like me at all. Even Hope raised her brows at me. "We'll take them inside."

I didn't stick around to wait for what he said. Instead, I spun and headed inside. The end-of-day bell was ringing, and the locker room would now be empty. Hope was trying to keep up with me, but I was on a mission to run away from my memories.

Having Cade back waged a war inside me. He'd been my first crush, but he was also a reminder of the one day in my life I tried my hardest to forget. He was a living, breathing, memory I couldn't escape.

"Jeez, Aria! Wait up."

I shook my head, and placed the goal outside the equipment room which sat between the two locker rooms. "Sorry." I flashed her a small smile, the most I could manage with my skin crawling. "Mom will probably be waiting for me."

Hope nodded like she understood, but I could see the doubt written all over her features. She knew when to push and when not to, and this was a time she shouldn't. I needed to process things and categorize them into their own little folders. Or find relief someway else.

We stayed silent as we headed into the locker room, got dressed, and headed out front together. Hope's bus was pulling into the lot as we got to the top of the stairs.

"I'll see you Monday!" she shouted, and with a

wave, she ran across the lot, faster than she had ever run in PE.

The lot was emptying of cars, but the one I wanted to see most wasn't there. I needed to get home and lock myself in my room to be able to take a full breath. I needed to breathe again. But Mom wasn't here. Her red car wasn't pulling into the lot, and the longer I stood on the steps, the more I wondered if she'd forgotten to pick me up.

I shot off a text to her and followed it up ten minutes later with a call, but it went unanswered. This wasn't the first time she'd been late, but if she didn't arrive within the next thirty minutes, I'd start walking.

Deciding to give my legs a rest, I plopped down on one of the top concrete steps and refreshed my cell constantly in case I'd missed a message. She'd worked the late shift last night, and Sal gave me a ride to school this morning, so it could only mean she'd worked the early shift today.

Mom and Sal were expanding the business and opening up a new diner, which meant they were gone more and more. If only I could pass my driving test. It wasn't as if I hadn't tried, because I had, I just...couldn't get it right. The control a car gave me scared the life out of me, and as soon as I sat behind the wheel, I froze. Nothing I did could stop it, so I'd decided for the rest of my life, I'd rely on rides and public transportation.

"Aria?"

I closed my eyes, wishing I hadn't heard his voice, but I couldn't deny it. His footsteps were coming closer, so I opened my eyes back up and turned my head to look at him, trying my hardest to paste a smile on my face. "Hey."

"What are you doing?" He moved down the steps so that, when he sat, his face was the same height as mine.

"Waiting for my ride."

He tilted his head to the side and looked around at the now nearly empty lot save for a couple of teachers' cars. It was Friday, which meant most of the teachers didn't stay late. They were as eager as the students to get home and start their weekends.

"Jan?" Cade asked, and I nodded in reply. He stared at me, blinking several times, and then stepped back. "Come on, I'll give you a ride."

"What?" I shook my head in refusal. "No, I'm good. I'll wait here—"

"Don't be stupid." He rolled his eyes, looking more like the sixteen-year-old I remembered than the mid-twenties man standing in front of me. "I'm heading that way anyway."

"You…are?"

"Yep." He puffed out his chest. "You're now looking at the proud owner of a three-bedroom home over on Wilmont."

"Wilmot." I choked out a laugh as I stood, my

body making the decision for me. "As in, the street two blocks away from my apartment?"

"The one and only." He held his arms out. "I'm gonna be your neighbor."

"Not sure you have the right definition of neighbor," I quipped as I met him at the bottom of the steps. "But sure, we'll go with that."

"You're too smart for your own good."

"Whatever you say, sir."

Cade's face screwed up as he stopped next to a sleek black car so shiny I could see my face reflected back at me in the bodywork. "That sounds downright disgusting coming from your mouth."

I fluttered my lashes and clasped my hands together, doing my best impression of the girls who had surrounded him on the field. "You don't like it, sir?"

"Ew." Cade shook his head as if to erase the words I'd spoken from his mind. He pointed at me from the opposite side of the car in warning. "Stop it."

"Or what?" I asked, pulling the door open when the lights flashed. "You gonna give me detention?"

Cade's nostrils flared, but the glint in his eyes told me he was playing. "Maybe I will, Miss Aria."

I pushed inside the car and tried to hold in my laughter. "You know that's not my last name, right?"

He turned the engine on and winked at me. "I know, but I kinda like the way it sounds."

I clicked my fingers and stared out the windshield as he pulled out of the parking spot. "Gotcha, kinda like how I call you sir."

"Exactly. Wait. No. Stop calling me that."

I grinned, so wide it actually hurt. "Okay, sir."

"Dammit, Aria. You're gonna be the death of me."

"Promises, promises."

———

CADE

I stared at the front of my new house. Mine. I owned an actual house. I wasn't sure this day was ever going to come, but now it was here, and it meant I was a real adult. The three-bedroom house was more than I needed for just me, but I couldn't turn it down at the price.

It was a fixer-upper. The siding needed to be replaced, the wood on the small porch needed sanding and varnishing, and the inside needed to be ripped out and started again. Between Dad and me, we'd already stripped out the kitchen and re-plastered all the walls. It was a blank canvas now, and today, the new kitchen was being installed by professionals, and the walls were being painted by Dad, Lola, Belle, Asher, and me.

"Did you know there are three bedrooms?" Belle

asked, sidling up next to me as I watched men carry cabinets into the house.

"There is?" I raised a brow, acting like I had no idea, and looked down at her not-so-innocent face.

"Yep." She pushed her flowing light-brown hair behind her ears with the palms of her hands.

"Hmmm." I nodded but said nothing else. I knew what she was going to say. The same thing she had since she found out I was moving back home.

Belle and I had always been close. There was a time I hated my dad for being with Lola. Hated that he was with a woman closer to my age than his. But it hadn't taken long for me to understand that what they had was different from what he'd had with my mom. It was so different: night and day.

As soon as Belle had come into this world, I knew I'd love her more than anything else. I hated that I had to move away to college when she was a toddler. At first, I'd come home on weekends, but by my senior year, my workload was so insane I only managed one out of every six.

I hated it. And I knew she hated it.

So as soon as I told her I was moving back home, she'd squealed and told me all about the plans for the room she would have at my house. And now I was guessing she'd already chosen which one she would claim as hers.

"I like the one with the view of the backyard,"

Belle continued, not unfazed by me being non-committal.

"Nope." I shook my head and held my hand out to her. Her small palm pressed against my large one, and then we walked up the short path lined with grass on one side and the driveway to the garage on the other. "That's my room."

She huffed. "Figures you'd take the one with its own bathroom."

"What can I say?" I shrugged and waved my arm at her when we got to the front door. "It's my house. I get to choose first."

"Fine." She placed her hand on her hip. "Then I want the second biggest one."

I held my hand out for her to shake and tried to keep my grin at bay. "Deal."

She shook my hand, her gaze not moving from mine. "No take-backs." With that, she let go, spun around, and ran down the hallway and toward the kitchen, shouting, "I've got my room picked out!"

I couldn't help the chuckle that escaped. There was no stopping Belle. She always knew what she wanted, and got exactly that one hundred percent of the time. She was a force to be reckoned with.

"You need to sign for this," a gruff voice said from behind me.

I turned around, coming face-to-face with one of the men who had carried in the supplies for the kitchen. It was more expensive than I'd anticipated to get exactly what I wanted, but thanks to the payout I'd received, I was able to afford it.

I didn't want to think about why I'd been given a payout. I didn't want to think about what I would have preferred instead of the money. I didn't want to go back to that night, not right now, not when I was holding a pen in my shaky hand about to sign the form to confirm they'd delivered the right things.

Once I'd scribbled my name, I handed the form back to him and then headed into the kitchen. Dad was already checking what they'd delivered as he spoke to one of the guys.

"Should have it all done by Tuesday. Water needs to be turned off until then."

Dad nodded and pushed his hand through his slightly graying hair. It had only appeared over the last couple of months, a few strands around his temple, but I thought it suited him.

"Sounds good to me," I said, and stepped forward, my attention focused on Dad and his dark-brown eyes. "I can get the bathroom stripped out in the meantime while the walls dry."

"Whatever you want, son." He stepped toward me, his face nearly level with mine. There was a time when he'd towered over me, but I'd soon caught up, and I was now an inch taller than him. "The guys and I will help any way we can."

"Thanks, Dad." I smiled and gazed around the

room. It was an empty shell right now, but I was hoping it would be all finished by the end of the month, and I could actually move in. Time couldn't go by fast enough.

"Cade!" Lola shouted from somewhere in the house. "Get your butt up here!"

Lola rarely shouted, but when she did, you knew you were in trouble. Dad and I both hesitated, neither of us wanting to be in the firing line.

"You first," Dad said, holding his arm out.

"Nu-uh"—I shook my head—"she's your wife. You first."

"Brody! I know you're down there too!"

"Shit," Dad cursed. He stared at me for a beat and then moved forward.

I followed him out of the kitchen and down the hallway toward the front door. The stairs sat opposite the door, right in the middle of the house. I loved the layout we'd created. From above, it almost looked like a lowercase n. The living room was to the left, the dining room to the right, and the kitchen was at the back, connecting it all. The rooms flowed into each other, exactly how I'd wanted it.

Upstairs was a different story. You were immediately greeted with the smallest bedroom, and next to that a bathroom. If you veered off to the left, you'd head into the master bedroom that looked out onto the backyard, but if you headed to the right, you'd get to what was now Belle's bedroom.

"Darlin'," Dad greeted. "What's with the shouting?"

Lola had her hand on one side of her hips and Asher on the other as she stood in the middle of the empty room. Her dark-brown hair rolled down her back in waves and whooshed to the side as she turned and pointed at the wall. "Look at what your daughter has done."

We all turned to face the wall that had *Belle's Room* written in big, black letters. A chuckle was working its way up my throat, and I had to do everything I could to keep it down.

"What?" Belle asked. "It's the truth."

"She's right," I said, stepping toward Belle. "I said she could have this room."

"That doesn't mean she can draw on the walls!" Lola groaned and let a squirming Asher down. He ran right to me, and I picked him up and threw him in the air. He clutched me around the neck, laughing.

"I want a room," he told me, his chocolate-brown eyes focused on me.

"You can share Belle's," I whispered, careful not to talk to loudly, but Belle heard me loud and clear.

"Nu-uh." She shook her head back and forth, her hair whipping her in the face. "This is my room."

"It's a huge room," I told her with a raised brow. "We can split it in half and decorate it however you want."

Belle looked away and narrowed her eyes around the room. "Can I paint it black?"

"Black?" Lola screeched. "Jes—"

"If you want." I shrugged and tickled Asher's stomach. "And you, big man?"

"Me big man."

"Yep." I nodded and ran my hand over his dark-brown hair. He looked so much like our dad already, and he was only four years old.

"Gween." He pointed at a wall. "I want gween gwass."

"You got it."

"I just can't even with you three," Lola said, her tone that of someone who was half fed up but she couldn't mask the smile building on her face.

"Me?" Dad asked, pointing at his chest.

"No." Lola looked up at him. "Those terrors." She hooked her thumb over her shoulder at us. "But don't even get me started on you, Brody Easton."

"Ohhhh, Dad's in trouble," Belle whispered, or at least tried to. With the room empty, her voice echoed off the walls.

Dad's brows lifted. "What did I do?"

"If you're asking that, then I'm not even going to bother telling you." She puffed out a breath. "I'm going to walk around to Jan and Aria's, see what they're getting up to and get away"—she waved her hand in the air—"from here."

"Aria?" Belle perked up. "I want to see Aria."

"Me too!" Asher screamed down my ear and squirmed to get down. The kid had no sense of danger and tried to leap from my arms.

"Of course you do," Lola said and held her hand out to Asher. "Come on, if you're good, I'll take you to get ice cream."

They both cheered as they exited, their chatter following them as they left the house. My new house was only a couple of blocks from Aria's apartment complex, so it would only take them a few minutes to get there.

I turned to look at Dad. "What did you forget?"

Dad grinned and stood next to me, staring at the graffiti on the wall. "Nothing. She just thinks I forgot it's our anniversary." He chuckled. "I'm taking her out for the night. Which reminds me, can you watch Belle and Asher?"

"Sure."

"If I only ever teach you one thing, let it be this, son." Dad gripped my shoulder, his features pulled into a serious expression. "Never forget birthdays or anniversaries."

"That's all you want me to know?"

"Yep. It'll save your life."

Chapter Four

ARIA

Wednesdays were family days. No matter what shift Mom was working, we always had a family meal. It had started out when I was six, and eleven years later, we continued the same tradition. The only difference now was that Sal joined us.

Today they were both working the late shift, which meant family dinner was at the diner. I didn't mind because it saved me trying to eat Mom's god-awful cooking. She tried to make the simplest of dishes but always failed. It didn't mean she gave up, though. I liked to think I got that kind of determination from my mom.

I'd barely sat down when my favorite flavor shake—banana—was placed in front of me from Mom. "How was school?" she asked, standing at the edge of the table. There were six sets of tables that fit four people around each, and when they had a party in here, all the tables were pushed together to create one giant one.

"School is school," I said with a shrug and reached for the straw in the shake. The banana creaminess exploded on my tongue, eliciting a groan from me. I took my fill of shake then leaned against the back of the black booth. "I have some homework to do."

Mom ran her hand through her dark-red hair, a look of concern on her face that vanished the moment Sal said, "What are we eating tonight? I'm starved."

Mom chuckled, but the pitch was off, her attention still zoned in on me. I hated when she stared at me like that. Like I was a bomb about to explode. I wasn't sure if she realized she made things a thousand times worse when she had that look in her eyes because all it did was make me feel even more guilty for who I was. For what I did. For who I'd allowed myself to become. She didn't understand what it was like being me, and I didn't need her to. I just needed her to not look at me like I was a stranger.

I hated being in my own skin sometimes, and right now, I itched for the relief I desperately needed—relief I'd been relying on more and more lately. Relief no one knew about. It wouldn't be long until I was out of the diner and on my way home, then I could give in to my cravings and allow myself a few seconds of freedom.

I stared at the giant clock on the wall and wished for the next couple of hours to fly by. All I needed to do was make small talk—give Mom the words she needed to hear so she could tell herself everything was perfect—and eat my food.

"I'll take the chicken and fries," I told Sal as I reached for my shake again. If I was drinking, I couldn't talk at the same time.

Mom told him what she wanted, and as he turned to place the order, the door flung open, and a head of light-brown hair whizzed into the diner, shouting, "Uncle Sal! Shake me!"

I snorted, which made my own shake shoot up the back of my throat and burn the back of my nose. My eyes watered and I coughed to try and get rid of the sensation, but it was no use, and by the time Belle was at our table, tears were streaming down my face.

"Aria? What's wrong?" Mom patted me on the back, probably thinking she was helping, but it really wasn't.

"Was someone mean to you?" Belle asked, her face now full of concern. For an eight-year-old, she sure acted like a mother hen sometimes.

Closing my eyes, I tried to sniff to stop the burning, not paying attention to anything around me until I opened my eyes back up and groaned. Belle wasn't on her own, nope, I couldn't have asked for small victories. She was flanked by Lola, Asher, and Uncle Brody, and of course, Cade.

"Aria is crying," Belle pointed out like it wasn't already obvious. Asher pulled himself up on the chair next to me, his small hand patting my arm.

"What's wrong?" Lola asked.

I croaked, "No—"

"I think someone was mean to her like Henry was to me," Belle supplied, planting her hands on her hips from the opposite side of the table.

"What?" Uncle Brody frowned. "That right, Jan?"

Mom choked on a laugh. "No, she was just—"

"Cade?" Uncle Brody didn't let Mom finish. "You knew someone was picking on Aria?"

"What?" Cade frowned. "I—"

"You're a teacher at that goddamn school, which means you look out for family. Aria is family."

I screwed up my nose, wishing I could become invisible and float away from this situation. The men in my life were anything but not protective. They went to bat for you even when you didn't need them to.

"I'm fine," I finally managed to get out. "Belle made me laugh when she waltzed in, and I snorted shake up my nose."

I was greeted with silence and several blinks, and then they were all laughing at me. Not with me, but at me, and I felt even worse than I had before. I hated being the center of attention, and now several sets of eyes in the diner were focused this way.

"Shakes are for drinking," Belle told me as if I hadn't already known. She pulled the chair out opposite me and sat down.

"I know," I told her, at the same time Sal placed a shake in front of her.

"You joining us?" Sal asked them.

"Sure," Uncle Brody said and pulled a table next to ours, not hesitating one bit.

"Wait." Lola held her hand in the air. "It's their family dinner night—"

"It's okay," Mom told her. "The more the merrier."

Sal took all their orders and walked back to the kitchen as everyone sat down. Uncle Brody and Lola sat on either side of Belle, and Mom pulled up a seat next to Lola, which meant there were two chairs left. One next to me, and one on the other side of Asher.

I kept my focus on Asher as he was handed some crayons and a picture to color in, intent on not paying attention to where Cade was going to sit, but it was no use. I was hyperaware of his movements and the shirt and pants he was wearing. He'd obviously come right from school too.

He pulled out the chair next to mine, sitting opposite his dad, and I pulled in a breath. I couldn't be this close to him. Being in the confines of his car a few days ago was bad enough, but with errant tears still trickling down my face and the embarrassment of the shake snorting, I couldn't cope with him only centimeters away. I felt like that same eight-year-old girl who had met him for the first time and fallen in love instantly.

"Hey," his deep voice greeted, his baritone low. "You okay?"

I nodded, too afraid to say an actual word to him, sure I would make the situation even worse.

Conversations surrounded us, but all the while, I stayed silent, not wanting to draw attention to myself. Asher handed me a green crayon and told me to color the grass, so I concentrated on my task at hand, and not on the person sitting beside me engrossed in his cell.

My skin itched for some kind of relief, my body craving something I shouldn't want, but it didn't matter. I knew I'd give in to it as soon as I was alone, and for a brief second, I'd feel like I was flying high. I didn't want to entertain the crash that would come after it—the low I'd experience— because those few seconds of euphoria were worth it.

I imagined gripping the object in my hand and leaning toward it, my breathing picking up as I did, and I completely forgot where I was until a hand touched my arm.

My head whipped around, my wide-eyed gaze landing on Cade. "Dad asked you a question."

I blinked, trying to clear the fog. "He did?" I shook my head, trying to evaporate all the warring thoughts, and moved my attention to Uncle Brody. "Sorry, I was miles away."

He smiled, the same kind of smile he gave Belle when he knew she was lying. "That's okay. I just asked if you'd thought about college yet."

The chatter around the table lowered, and I could feel the burn of Mom's gaze on the side of my face. We hadn't talked much about what would happen when I finished my senior year. I knew she wanted me to get out of this place and away from all the memories surrounding us, but I wasn't sure what I wanted.

"I...I'm not sure I'm going to go to college," I murmured.

"What?" It was Cade whose tone was one of disbelief. "You have a 3.8 GPA. Of course you should go to college."

I shrugged, thankful I could see our food being brought to the table. "I don't even know what I'd do in college. I'm not..." I trailed off, not wanting to say the rest. I wasn't going to reveal myself to everyone around this table, not when I wouldn't admit it to myself. I'd keep my worries inside and let them out the way I normally did: alone.

Thankfully, the conversation was interrupted by

our plates being placed in front of all of us, and Sal finally sat on the other side of Asher. I leaned over to help cut up Asher's food.

"You could get a scholarship," Mom announced, and I flicked my gaze up to her. She hadn't touched her food yet, her focus not waning from me. "You said you'd try out for track this year," she reminded me.

I gritted my teeth and stared into her eyes. I had said I would try out for track, but that was before I knew Cade would be the coach.

"You're trying out for track?" Cade asked, but I couldn't answer him. I couldn't form any words.

"She is," Mom told him for me. "Are you the coach this year?"

I felt Cade shuffle in his seat, his arm a whispering touch against mine, and I pulled in a sharp breath. "I am. Tryouts are next week."

Mom smiled up a storm as she said, "Aria will be there."

Everyone started to murmur between themselves, but I couldn't do anything but look down at my food and try to regulate my breathing. She'd spoken for me, and I hated that, but I wouldn't call her out. I was the kind of person who kept it inside and let it go, but it didn't mean it wouldn't eat away at me.

Running was something I did for me, not for anyone else, and the fact that my legs were shorter than most of the girls on the track team would probably mean I wouldn't come anywhere close to their times. Maybe I wouldn't even make the team.

My feet bobbed up and down on the floor as I resisted the urge to bite my fingernails. I was on the brink of something, I just didn't know exactly what it was.

A hand landed on my knee, large fingers gripping it to stop my momentum. I swallowed as my breathing picked up, but didn't turn to face Cade.

"You're making the table shake," he whispered in my ear, his breath fanning across my neck. I hated that it made me shiver, hated that having his hand on me soothed all my crazy thoughts instantly. One touch shouldn't be able to calm me the way it had.

"Sorry," I croaked out, turning to look at him. His dark-blue eyes shone bright, but this close, I could see the starburst of green around his pupil. "I just…" I didn't know what I was going to say to him. His hand was still on my knee, his thumb rubbing back and forth. "I want to go home," I finally managed to say, not shying away from the truth.

He blinked, something swirling in his gaze, and then he nodded. He didn't look away. Instead, he kept his attention on me, almost as if he were searching for something. My heart hammered in my chest, and my fingers itched to reach out and run across the slight stubble lining his jaw. For the first time since he'd left for college, I didn't feel so...*invisible*. They said the eyes were the gateway to the soul, and I never believed it until this very moment.

I wasn't sure what was swirling between us, but when Uncle Brody said, "What do you think, Cade?" It broke whatever spell we had both been under. His hand snapped back from my knee, and he stopped looking at me. I craved to pull him back around, to stare into his eyes again, but it was gone, like everything else in my life.

I was alone...again.

———

ARIA

It wasn't easy to carry a thirty pound four-year-old, up the stairs while trying to follow a tired eight-year-old, but I was managing just fine.

Asher was dead asleep, and had been for the last twenty minutes, propped up against my arm on the sofa. He hadn't moved from his spot next to me since Lola and Brody left for their monthly date night, not even when I answered the door to the pizza delivery.

I always let them stay up a little later when I babysat, and I was sure Brody and Lola thanked me for it because it meant they got to stay in bed a little longer the next morning.

Belle made her way to her room, and I whispered, "I'll be back in a minute. Get your pj's on, okay?"

"Okay," she murmured back in her tired voice.

I moved to the door opposite Belle's and entered the pirate-themed room. Asher was obsessed with anything to do with the sea, but mainly pirates, which meant he had a hand-built bed from his uncle Ford that resembled a ship, and there was a mural painted on one of his walls. It was the perfect room for a little boy, and even I'd admit I was kind of jealous.

Luckily, I'd already changed him into his pj's, so all I had to do was place him in his bed and tuck him in. I ran my hand through his soft, brown hair, and smiled. He looked so peaceful. I wondered if I ever looked like that anymore. I was always wound so tight, afraid of someone noticing something I didn't want them to see, that I constantly had my guard up.

I stared at Asher for another couple of seconds, switched his nightlight on, and then exited his room. Belle was already in bed when I walked into her room, the covers up to her chin, and her half-closed eyes focused on her bedroom door.

"Read to me?" she asked, although she didn't

need to because this was our routine whenever I was here.

I lifted the book she held against her chest and shuffled onto the edge of her bed, settling in for a couple of chapters of *The Faraway Tree*. This was one of my favorites when I was Belle's age, and I could remember my dad reading it to me, doing all the different voices and getting excited at parts. He always read it like it was the first time he'd come across the words in that order, but I knew he'd read it over and over again.

Belle's soft snores rang out after a few pages, but I didn't move for several minutes. I stayed put, listening to the quiet sounds of the house, and wondered why I always felt so…*different* when I was here. I'd spent more time here than my own apartment growing up, and it had always felt like a second home.

Maybe it was because these walls didn't hold the memories my apartment walls did.

I always found myself in this exact position, hating the thought of going home and being alone again. Mom and Sal were working the late shift, which meant they wouldn't be home until around 2 a.m. And when they got home, they'd only have a few hours before one of them would be opening up for the morning shift.

Sometimes I wished we had more of a…*normal* life. One where we all ate together around the kitchen table at dinner and talked about our day. We weren't normal, though. None of what we'd been through was normal.

The front door opening and closing brought me out of my own head, and I slowly lifted off Belle's bed. I placed a piece of paper in the book to mark the page and then headed down the stairs. It was early for Brody and Lola to be home.

"Brody got called in to work on a case," Lola said.

"Oh." I nodded like I understood, and part of me did. There had been times over the years he'd been called away on a job at a moment's notice, and he'd have to leave without more than a quick goodbye.

Lola patted the seat next to her on the sofa. "Come sit." I did as I was told and stared as she flung her heels off her feet. "God, I hate those things." She groaned and rubbed her feet. "I wasn't sure I could last another hour in them."

I laughed because the thought of wearing something like that didn't appeal to me, no matter how much Mom went on about me needing a pair for winter formal. I had no intention of going, but if she had her way, she'd come with me.

"You doing okay, sweetheart?" Lola asked.

Her question took me by surprise. "Me?" I pointed at my chest and feigned a smile. "Yeah, I'm good."

She tilted her head to the side. "You sure? You know you can always talk to me, right?"

I swallowed past the building lump in my throat. It was on the tip of my tongue to spill everything to her, to let it all out and bleed my pain, but I couldn't. I couldn't tell her what I did in the privacy of my own bedroom. I couldn't tell her the relief I itched for. I couldn't tell anyone.

"I know," I whispered, trying to keep my emotions in check. "I'm good. Really."

She stayed silent for a few seconds as she leaned back on the sofa. Her features relaxed, but her eyes told a different story. "It's not weird having Cade as a teacher?"

I blinked. And then I blinked again. "Erm...I guess." I shrugged. "I haven't seen him for years, so…"

"He's changed," Lola said. "He's not the same happy-go-lucky sixteen-year-old he was when you first met him."

"He's not." I shook my head and started to construct the wall around me. I didn't want to talk about this. I didn't want to—

"Neither are you, Aria." I swallowed at her words. "I know it's hard that he's your teacher, but he's still part of our family. Your family." We'd always been one extended family, never separate entities, but she'd never know how alone I always felt. You could be surrounded by a thousand people and still be the loneliest person in the world. "Family always comes first."

I heard her words loud and clear, but the fact of the matter was, I wasn't really part of her family. My family had been ripped apart nine years ago. One action had changed the course of my entire life, and I'd not realized how much impact one moment could have until then.

Lola leaned her head back on the sofa and stared over at me. She was always good at reading people. She knew when to push, and knew when to let something go. Tonight, she was letting it go. "Wanna stay here tonight? I don't know when Brody will be back, and Cade is at his new house for the weekend." She stuck out her bottom lip, acting nothing like the twenty-nine-year-old she was. "I don't want to be on my own."

I shook my head, but my lips were spreading into a grin. "I got nothing better to do."

"Good, because I'm in the mood for a chick flick and no one else will watch them with me."

I stood. "I'll make some popcorn."

"This is why I love you!" Lola shouted after me, and that feeling of home washed over me again.

Maybe it wasn't the place. Maybe it was the people. Either way, I'd savor the time I was here because, as soon as I was back in my apartment, the feeling would evaporate faster than raindrops on a scorching day.

———————

CADE

Dad: The guys are coming over. We're
having a cookout. Bring beer.

I chuckled at the message from my dad and looked
down at the paintbrush I was holding. The repairs
on the house were nearly complete, and the inside
was done, which left only the outside. The siding
needed a fresh coat of paint, and then I'd be
finished, which was what I was doing at 10 a.m. on
a Saturday morning.

I'd already been out for a run and sorted out my
homework for the weekend so I'd be prepared for
the week ahead. Now that the extracurricular activi-
ties were up and running, my hours during the
school day wouldn't be as free as they had been.

Dad: Lola said to pick up hamburger
meat too.

I shook my head and typed out a reply to Dad:

Cade: You sure it isn't you that's meant to
get meat?

I waited for his reply and grinned when it came through.

Dad: See you in an hour.

I tucked my cell back into my pocket and finished painting the slat of wood a light blue. Every weekend I'd been at the house, trying to finish all the repairs it needed, so I was sure I could give myself a break today. My official move-in date was next weekend, but all I was waiting on was my furniture to be delivered, and I could manage without a sofa and television for a few days. Once all my supplies were put away, I headed inside for a shower.

My cell pinged again as I pushed my feet into my sneakers and positioned my sunglasses on my face.

Lola: Could you grab some juice boxes for the kids on the way over? Your dad said you're getting beers.

I grabbed my keys, walked outside, and locked the door behind me.

Cade: On it.

I still couldn't believe I had my own house. The

years had flown by, but inside, I still felt like the fifteen-year-old kid who listened to his parents argue over who had cheated on who first.

The drive to the store near my dad's house took me past the street I grew up on. The first fifteen years of my life, my mom had basically been a single parent. It was simply the way we'd lived, and Mom didn't seem too bothered by it. Until the year I turned sixteen. That year changed everything. It was the year I met Lola, who tutored me, the year my dad cheated on my mom, and the year I found out my mom had done the same.

And then I'd gotten shot.

I winced as I drove toward Dad and Lola's, remembering the pain I'd been in. Lola had been pregnant with Belle at the time, and I hadn't thought twice about diving in front of the bullet for her. That day was full of sadness and chaos, but a smile worked its way on my lips as the memory of a bossy Aria came into view. That had been the first time I met her, and I'd never forgotten her lopsided pigtails and her overalls rolled up at the ankles because of how small she was.

Mom moved to France after that, and I'd only seen her a handful of times since. She married twice after Dad, each marriage lasting no more than two years, and if the invitation I received last week was anything to go by, she was getting hitched again to some multimillionaire French socialite. Mom never did anything by halves. Part of me wanted to blame my dad for the life she was leading now, but it wasn't all on him.

My last three years of high school, Dad got a promotion and was home more. Things had changed. Change wasn't always a bad thing, and in our case, it was exactly what we had needed. It meant I truly got to know my dad and build the father-and-son relationship I was always seeking growing up.

Several cars littered the driveway, which meant Dad's team was here, otherwise known as the uncles I'd grown up with. They'd always been there to protect and guide me, but it hadn't been them I'd wanted when I learned how to ride a bike. It was my dad I wished was there to cheer me on, not the men he saw as his family, but it was the way it was, and there was nothing I could do to change it now.

Switching the car off, I tried to shake all my thoughts. I didn't want to go into a happy house with a cloud of the past hanging over me.

I could hear the laughter before I even opened up the front door, and as soon as I did, Asher came running toward me with a helmet on his head. I jumped out of the way just in time and pushed the front door shut with my foot.

"Hey, Asher?" He turned toward me, his little face screwed up. "Slow down there, bud."

"Can't." He dipped down, preparing to tackle

something else. "Gotta get the bad guys." He took off in a whirlwind, and I followed after him into the kitchen.

"Hey," I greeted Lola. She stood at the kitchen counter, prepping food. "I got your stuff." I placed it all on the opposite counter and stepped back. "Dad and the guys outside?" I asked, trying to see through the sliding glass door that led out into the backyard.

"Yep." Lola huffed out a breath and swiped her hand over her forehead. "Could you go tell Belle to come down and help set the table?"

"Sure." I planted a kiss on Lola's cheek and exited the kitchen. Lola was only a few years older than me, and although she was technically my step-mom, she was more like an older sister. She was now a constant in my life, along with my dad and two siblings.

I took the stairs two at a time and turned left at the top to go to Belle's bedroom. "Belle?" I called, but I didn't get a response, so I walked inside her room and stumbled back when she jumped out of nowhere. "Jesus!"

"Scared you!" Her giggle took over her whole body as she caved in on herself, and I couldn't miss an opportunity like this, so I dived forward and tickled her.

"Stop! Stop!" she screamed and laughed.

"Only when you declare me the winner!" I said,

and threw her over my shoulder, not stopping the ticklefest.

"Fine!" She squealed as I let her down to the ground. "You're the winner." Her face was bright red from all the laughing, and her hair was a wild mess sticking up in all different directions. She tried to move it out of her eyes as she crossed her bedroom.

"Your mom said you need to go and set the table." I started to turn around, just as I caught sight of something out of the corner of my eye. *What the hell...*

"Put your hands up!" Belle shouted, widening her stance and holding me at ransom with a water gun.

I flung my hands in the air, surrendering to her. The girl was a terror. "Your mom will kill you if you use that in here."

Belle's eyes narrowed, and then she pressed the trigger, soaking me and the line of teddy bears beside me. She was relentless and didn't stop until the water gun was empty. Water dripped over my face, down my chest, and in the time it took me to wipe my face, she'd raced past me.

"I'll get you back for this!" I shouted after her as her feet stomped down the stairs.

Shaking my head, I walked into my bedroom and pulled my T-shirt over my head as I pushed the door open and then slammed it behind me. The kid was a menace, and I had no doubt she'd be a handful as a teenager. *Good luck with that, Dad.*

I threw the T-shirt into my hamper, murmuring under my breath ideas on how to get her back. She's started a war, and now I had to put an end to it. My chest was still wet, so I spun to get a towel when something caught my eye. It wasn't an eight-year-old girl holding me at ransom this time, though. It was a pair of jeans on the floor, alongside some sneakers, which were definitely *not* mine.

I tilted my head to the side as I stared at them, trying to work out what the hell was going on, when a throat cleared from behind me. My eyes widened as I spun around, and blinked several times, sure I was seeing things.

"Aria?"

She sat in my bed, her eyes puffy and hair even wilder than Belle's. "Huh?" She rubbed her hands over her face, trying to wake herself up. Her gaze roved over me, starting at my sneakers, up and over my shorts, and finally my bare chest.

I wasn't sure she even realized she was cataloging everything, but I couldn't deny the way my body buzzed at her attention. She was in my bed, staring at me like I was her next meal, and I could do nothing but stand here perfectly still, too afraid to move even an inch in case it brought her out of her trance.

Her gaze finally settled on my face, and it

brought her out of her daze. "Oh my god!" She flung the covers aside and jumped out of bed. "I'm sorry, Cade." She was talking, saying something, but I wasn't listening to a single word she was saying. All I could focus on was where her T-shirt stopped high on her thighs, concealing just enough to keep her modesty but making my body burn with the need to find out what it covered.

I shouldn't have been thinking about her like that. I shouldn't have been looking at her the way I was. But fuck…

She was standing in front of me half-naked, just like I was.

I couldn't help myself.

My feet carried me forward, and I wasn't sure whether it was the darkness in the room or the fact we were alone in a place that was mine. "What are you doing in here, Aria?" I asked, my voice deeper than usual. She was getting to me more than I cared to admit.

"I…" She bit down on her bottom lip, and I heard her quick inhale of breath as I halted a foot in front of her. Her head tilted back so she could stare up at me. Her T-shirt slid up, and I nearly groaned when more of her creamy skin showed, peeking at me, tempting me more than anything else ever had. "I slept here last night."

"In my bed?" I was fighting every instinct I had

not to press my body against hers, but I was starting to lose control.

Aria nodded in reply to my question, but she didn't make a single move. Could she feel the air swirling between us? I couldn't have been imagining this, it just wasn't possible.

"Do you do that often?" My voice was practically a whisper, but the thought of her sleeping in my bed had me irrationally fired up. How many times had she slept on my sheets and then I'd slept on them the night after? How many times had her red hair been spread over my pillows?

"Only when I stay over," she said, her voice small and unsure. I was towering over her. Maybe I was scaring her?

Shit.

What the hell was I doing?

Not only was she seventeen, but she was my goddamn student, and I was here staring her down and licking my lips like she was here for me, and me only.

I needed to get away from her.

As far away as humanly possible.

Chapter Five

ARIA

"And, I swear to god, he was the best kisser ever."

Hope's words vibrated through my head, but I wasn't really listening to any of them. She'd talked nonstop about her amazing weekend with her sister and their band and all the hot guys she'd met backstage. Hope wasn't the kind of person who liked to stay home on her own, so she preferred to be around people than alone. I didn't understand it because alone was my favorite place to be. Her life was so different from mine, and sometimes I wished I was her. She didn't have a care in the world, or at least that was how she made it seem.

"But then he got a little too handsy if you know what I mean." She elbowed me in the side, but I kept my gaze trained on the bustling school hallway. "Aria? Are you listening to me?"

"Huh?" I whipped my head around to face her, blinking several times in quick succession. "Yeah, yeah, he was the best kisser but then got too handsy."

She sighed. "He was so hot too. Maybe I should have lost my V-card then and there." She paused as I stopped at my locker to switch out my books. "What do you think?"

I closed my locker, the scrape of the metal making me cringe. Everything had me on edge today. I'd woken feeling a little weird, and not really with it. It was like the edges of my vision were constantly blurry. "I think you should have offered it on a silver platter to him."

Hope blinked, her brows rising, and I tried to keep my face pulled into a serious mask, but I was failing epically. "Oh hardy har, you're so funny."

"Thanks." I hugged my books to my chest and leaned against the locker, able to feel like I could finally take a full breath. Hope always managed to make me think about anything else but what was whirring around in my head. There was only a minute or two until our next class, a class I still wasn't sure whether I dreaded or anticipated. My feelings were all over the damn place, and it was all down to one person: Cade.

"Seriously though, you need to listen to your gut if you—"

A gruff laugh cut me off, and I swung my gaze toward the door to my right. I knew who it would be before he stepped out of his classroom, but I hadn't expected a woman to follow him out. A woman who looked familiar.

I couldn't move my attention off them as she whipped her hair to the side and placed her hand on his arm. My skin crawled as I watched her touch him, and I couldn't help but wonder if he liked it. Was she the kind of woman he had always dated? The obviously beautiful kind?

"Isn't that Miss Simmons?" Hope asked, and I narrowed my eyes on them.

It *was* Miss Simmons, aka Jasmine's big sister. The same Jasmine who we avoided at all costs. The same Jasmine who liked to fling names at me like it was a sport. The same Jasmine who hated me for no apparent reason.

"Yep," I said. Cade's gaze met mine, and his dark-blue eyes flashed with something I couldn't place. I wondered whether he was thinking about Saturday. Was he remembering how close we'd been in his bedroom? Was he thinking about the way we'd talked like we used to, and laughed like we did when we were younger? But the look was gone in an instant as he stared back down at Miss Simmons.

"I better head to class."

"Same," Hope groaned. "Band rehearsal at my place tonight. Call me later?"

"You got it."

I pushed off the locker and pulled back my shoulders. Being afraid wasn't my MO. At least, I tried not to let it be. All I had to do was make it through to the end of the school year. Then I'd be out of this hellhole and able to start my life without the past dragging me down.

"Good afternoon, Mr. Easton," I said, my voice sickly sweet. I even fluttered my eyelashes for good measure. He'd told me he hated when I called him that, and I was in the kind of mood to get under his skin. Maybe I was looking for a reaction? Or maybe I just liked to annoy him.

"Aria." He nodded and kept his face straight, but I noticed the small quirk of his lips. I knew he hated those words coming out of my mouth, but he didn't have a choice because, here, he was my teacher. It didn't matter I'd known him for more than half of my life.

"I'm sorry, Miss…" He trailed off, obviously not having a clue who the woman in front of him was. I bit down on my bottom lip to keep my grin at bay.

"Simmons," Miss Simmons replied. "But you can call me Willow."

"Like the tree?" Cade blurted out, and I couldn't hold in my snort. He'd never been one for mincing his words, and I was one hundred percent sure he didn't have a brain-to-mouth filter.

Her smile dropped a fraction, but she perked right back up and pushed her chest out. "Exactly."

"Right." Cade's gaze slid back to mine as the bell rang out. "I better head inside and teach the youth of today."

Miss Simmons giggled, and I finally spun around, screwing my face up at the way her voice tried to lure him in. Did that actually pick up men?

I headed to my usual seat and placed my books on the table. We were three weeks into senior year, and everyone was talking about college applications and what they were going to study. Football players were showing off the number of colleges that had written to them, and the cheerleaders were eating up every second of it.

I had no idea what I was going to do. Track tryouts were in a couple of days, and even though Mom had told Cade I'd be trying out, part of me wanted to deny her. But what good would that do? Maybe track would be the answer to everything, plus I'd get in extra running time to keep my thoughts at bay.

My gaze continually drifted to the clock, and I watched the seconds tick by. This was my last class of the day, and as soon as I was done, I could go home, get into my bed, and sleep the evening away. It was a tactic I'd taken to doing when I didn't want to be in the world around me. It wasn't that I wanted to leave it completely. I just…needed a break. I needed to reset, and it was part of my process. If I allowed myself to give in to my cravings constantly, it would never work. I'd given in six days ago, but I was determined to at least make it to seven days this time.

One day. All I needed was one more day, and then I could finally scratch the itch burning inside of me.

The bell rang, and I jumped out of my skin. I'd been so far in my own head, I hadn't even realized school was almost over. The students filed out of the room and spilled into the hallways. I waited an extra second, shook my head, and then stood.

"Aria?" Cade called, but when I looked over at him, his attention was on his laptop. "I need a word."

I nodded even though he couldn't see me, and pushed my books into my bag. Mom had texted me to tell me Sal would be picking me up, which meant I couldn't make him wait long because I knew he'd be heading back to the diner afterward.

"Sir?" I asked, my lips quirking on one side as he raised his brow and finally gave me his attention.

"Hate that," he murmured, then stood to his full height, towering over me. "Tryouts are in two days. I didn't see your name on the list." He crossed his arms over his chest and stared me down.

"You know that doesn't work on me, right?" I circled my finger in the air to point at his face. He narrowed his eyes even more, and if I were anyone else, I'd probably be shitting my pants, but I was Aria, the girl who watched on the sidelines as he practiced his lacrosse. The girl who laughed when he jumped at a scary part in a movie.

"What about now?" he asked, and I couldn't hold in the chuckle dying to break free.

"Nope." I tilted my head to the side. "You just look like a pissed-off teddy bear."

He gasped and slapped his palm against his chest. "I'm offended."

I rolled my eyes. "No, you're not." My breath left me in a whoosh, and I spun around. "See you tomorrow, Mr. Easton."

His footsteps followed behind me, but I hadn't expected his hand to wrap around my arm and stop my momentum. His fingers curled all the way around, meeting each other, and I couldn't help but stare down at them.

I flicked my gaze up to his face, but he was staring at his hand too. I wasn't sure what the frown on his face meant, but he didn't let go as he looked up at me. "Try out for the team, Aria."

"Why?" I asked. Why was he so insistent?

"Because I've watched you run. Your mom is right. You could get a scholarship."

"Have you been stalking me?" It was meant to

come out light and fluffy, but my voice betrayed me. The thought of him watching me made me feel like that same eight-year-old girl with a crush all over again.

"So what if I have." He stepped closer, his hand tightening on my arm. I wasn't even sure he was aware he was doing it. "Try out, Aria. You have nothing to lose."

He was right. I didn't have anything to lose, because I'd already lost it all.

———

ARIA

I stood on the sidelines and jumped up and down on the spot, warming my body up. I'd never run competitively, always doing it to find an escape, but this could change everything. If I made it onto the team, it could potentially take me away from this place. It could start something good in my life. But it could also make my escapism disappear.

Running was always my first port of call, but it was *never* my last. I used it as a buffer to stop myself from doing what I really wanted to, but it only worked half of the time. The other half I gave in. I let my body and mind have what it craved so much: silence. It was all I wanted. A reprieve from everything rolling around in my head. The memories, the images so vivid…

It was almost as if I were back there.

"They'll never be able to get us once we've finished," Dad's *high-pitched voice told me. There was something off about him, and as soon as he came into my room and told me we had to go to the store, I knew I had to go along with what he was saying.*

He opened up another box of aluminum foil and attached it to the kitchen window. He'd covered every single surface, and all that was left now was this window and the apartment door.

"Tape," Dad demanded, and I pulled some off for him *and handed it over.* *"I'll always keep you safe, Aria."* *He stared down at me and held his hand out for more tape. His light-brown eyes were the same shade as mine, but right then, they looked so different.*

Like there was something missing.

"I want all of you to run around the track five times."

Cade's voice interrupted my thoughts, and I stumbled back a little. I was heading down the dark path again, and I was scared of what would find me at the end of it. It was so easy to lose myself in the memories, and it was happening more and more lately, almost as if they were haunting me, trying to pull me back in and not let me go.

"Remember to pace yourselves," Cade continued.

I tried to shake all of my thoughts and concentrate on what was in front of me: tryouts. Cade stood at the start line, his arm raised as we all lined up. I didn't know most of the girls trying out for the track team, but one face I was more than familiar with: Jasmine. She was a cheerleader, so why the hell was she trying out for track?

Cade blew the whistle, and everyone took off. Some of them sprinted, others paced themselves, and I was right in the middle. It only took one trip around the track for me to zone in and lose myself to the rhythm of my feet slapping the ground. The more I ran, the easier it was to forget about the images in my head. Each beat set me off higher, and by the time I'd finished the fourth lap, there were only two girls in front of me.

I still had plenty of gas left in my system, so I took my time until I got to the halfway mark, and then I sprinted. I darted past one girl who was sweating so much she looked like she was having a shower. And I was only a few paces behind the girl in front of me as we both passed the finish line.

"Well done," she said, her breath coming out in pants. It was obvious she was used to running like this.

"Thanks," I replied and planted my hands on my hips, slowing down to a walk so I didn't shock my muscles with stopping dead.

"I didn't know you could run like that." I finally took a proper look at her. I recognized her as a junior who had transferred here last year. She was at least four inches taller than me, and her legs were definitely that of a runner. Her short black hair was held off her face with a headband, and her straight nose led to dark-brown eyes. "You should have tried out sooner."

I shrugged, not really wanting to overshare. "I normally only run for me."

She nodded like she understood, but she couldn't. No one ever could. "I get that." She held her hand out to me. "I'm Reagan."

I placed my hand in hers. "Aria."

"Girls!" Cade shouted, and we both turned to look at him. He waved his arm, indicating for us to come back to him, so Reagan and I walked side by side toward him. I couldn't help but beam at the grin on his face.

"You can both get changed and meet me in my office."

The smile dropped from my face, a frown replacing it as I wondered what that meant. There were still girls trying out, and we were being sent to get changed. It didn't make sense.

"But—"

Reagan grabbed my arm and pulled me with her as she walked away from him and across the field. "It's a good thing," she told me.

"It is?" I asked as we entered the locker rooms. I was only using them because it was after school, but had I known Jasmine was trying out, I would have gone to the bathrooms instead.

"Yeah." Reagan moved toward a locker on the right side of the room. "It means he doesn't need to see anything else from us." She grinned and pulled her running shorts off. "It means we're in."

"Really?" I couldn't help but stare at her like she had two heads. I'd never been chosen for anything, but maybe that was because I'd never tried out. I'd kept myself locked away, preferring to disappear into the shadows. That way, I could go by unnoticed.

"Yep." Reagan walked by me and into the showers, leaving me standing in the middle of the locker room with my mouth opening and closing like a fish. "Get changed!" Reagan shouted at me. "He wants to see us in his office."

Right. Yeah. I shook my head and opened up the locker I was using. I forwent the shower, not wanting to expose myself to anyone, and changed back into my jeans and T-shirt. I was pushing my running shoes into my backpack when the doors opened and all the other girls filed in, including Jasmine.

I didn't give her the chance to say anything. Instead, I slung my backpack over my shoulder and walked out. Reagan was waiting outside Cade's office, and as I got a couple of feet away, Cade came in off the field.

"Come in, girls," he said, his rough voice washing over me. We followed him inside, and Cade pointed to the seats against the back wall, but I opted to stand as he leaned against his desk. His hand curled around the edge, his long fingers drumming against the wood. "You're both on the team." Cade didn't look at me as he said it, and I couldn't help but wonder why. Why was he staring at Reagan and giving her all his attention? And more importantly, why was I noticing?

"Thanks, Coach," Reagan said, but I couldn't get my mouth to work.

"The schedule isn't going to be easy," Cade warned, "but that's because I know you can make it to state."

"We can?" I asked, my words coming out broken.

Cade nodded and stood, but still, he didn't look at me. "You can. I'll get your class schedule tonight and work out training times. Pick them up from me tomorrow."

Reagan nodded and stood, walking by me, accepting his dismissal. I started to turn to follow her out, but Cade calling out, "Aria?" stopped me.

"Yeah?" I slid my gaze to his, and for the first time since I entered his office, I felt like I could breathe.

"You did amazing." His lips lifted into a genuine smile, and I felt it all the way down to my toes. My stomach fluttered with butterflies at the way he was looking at me, and I remembered the way he'd stared down at me in his room. Something had happened in that moment. I wasn't sure what, but it was *something*.

"I did?"

"Yeah." He tilted his head to the side, his teeth now showing because his smile was so big. "You fuckin' did."

I quirked my lips and pulled my bag tighter against my shoulders. "Thanks, Coach."

His features screwed up. "Not sure what I hate more coming out of your mouth: sir or coach."

I laughed, feeling all of the tension I'd been carrying evaporate. "How about Coach Cade?"

He shook his head and looked down at his desk, shuffling through some papers. "Get out of here, you terror. I'll see you in the morning."

"Aye aye, Captain."

His groan was the last thing I heard as I practically skipped out of his office and out of school.

———

CADE

It felt weird to sit in a teachers' lounge. Part of me felt like I was an intruder, and still the eighteen-year-old kid I used to be, which was why I spent most of my free time working in my office near the gym.

But today, I'd needed a change. I needed to switch it up.

As soon as I poured myself a coffee and sat down, Willow Simmons was on me. I wanted to tell her she was coming on mighty strong, but part of me liked the attention.

Back in college, I'd loved every bit of attention the girls gave me, but the last couple of years had been different. I no longer wanted to hang out with women who didn't mean anything to me. I didn't want the one-night stands.

Everything had changed after *that* night: the way I thought, and the way I lived my life. They said everything happened for a reason, and I wasn't going to waste the reason I was still here. The reason blood still flowed through my veins. The reason air still expanded my chest. I'd been given a second chance, and I had to live it. And not only for myself but for the three people who'd had life snatched away from them.

"Cade, right?"

I nodded and flashed Willow a smile. "Yep."

"Mind if I sit?" Willow asked, pointing down at

the chair next to me, already halfway down into the seat.

"Sure." I waved my hand at it and took a sip of my coffee. We only had ten minutes until the first class of the day, and I was looking forward to it, unlike the other teachers in this room. As soon as I heard their murmurings about when the next vacation was, I remembered one of the reasons why I'd steered clear of this room in the first place.

"You just moved here, right?"

I raised a brow and looked at Willow. "Moved back, yeah. I grew up here. Went to this school actually."

"Really?" Her false eyelashes fluttered as she batted her eyelids. "Wow. I can't imagine teaching in my old high school."

I grinned because I understood. The plan was to never come back here and teach, but life liked to throw curveballs at you. You could either stand in its way and get yourself knocked out, or you could move to the left and start over. I decided to start over, even if it was where I'd begun.

"It is what it is," I said, not really interested in going over my life history. She only needed to know the basics.

Willow placed some of her light-brown hair behind her ear and quirked her lip on one side. I knew the signs better than anyone else. She was trying to gain my attention, but the low V cut of her blouse showcasing her cleavage didn't do it for me.

"So I guess that means you know about Clive's bar?"

I chuckled and shuffled forward on my seat, more than ready to get out of here. "I do."

"We all meet up there on Fridays after school. You should join us."

"Maybe." I flicked my gaze around the room and took stock of everyone. They ranged in age, the oldest being my old chemistry teacher who had to be pushing seventy now, and the youngest being… well, probably Willow and me. I wasn't sure how old she was, but at twenty-five, I was the young guy—the one who "didn't understand" what twenty years in the job did to you. I called bullshit.

"We have a blast," Willow continued as she settled back in her seat and crossed her legs. Her skirt rode up her thigh, flashing her tan skin. "Last week Harold got so drunk we had to call his wife to come get him at nine." She giggled. "He's such a lightweight."

I had no idea who Harold was.

All my old high school friends had moved away and not come back, which meant I didn't have any real friends to just…hang out with. I was a loner, but I'd never been that way. My family surrounded me, but I needed more than that. I needed someone to go and shoot the shit with and drink a beer. I needed a social life, and this would be the start of that.

Mind made up, I stood. "What time do you meet there?"

Willow's smile spread so wide I was sure she was going to break her face. "Between seven and eight."

I nodded. "Okay, I'll think about it." I hooked my thumb over my shoulder. "Better get to class."

Willow huffed out a breath. "Ugh, that time of day again."

"Yep," I replied. She was like most of the other people in this room. She didn't want to be here, but I *needed* to be here, for more reasons than I liked to admit.

Chapter Six

ARIA

It wasn't often I worked a shift in the diner, but when I got here for our weekly family dinner, and Mom told me they were two people down, I didn't really have a choice in the matter.

I'd been put on pot duty, which meant my hands were constantly wet and covered in suds, but at least the dishwasher was working for half of my shift. I was four hours in, and it was already 9 p.m. I should have been back at the apartment doing homework and checking out my new workout schedule, but instead, I was here, in the one place I hated.

When I was a little girl, I'd come here and happily sit in a booth while people came in and out to eat food or drink a shake. But over the years, I'd started to resent the place. It was the reason my mom was at home less and less, and the reason I was alone most of the time. I wanted out of this place so I could choose something better for myself. I had no idea what that something better was, but it would be more than this. I couldn't stay here and become my mom. I loved her more than anything, but I hated the fact she'd settled.

Even when Dad was here, he didn't work the way Mom did. He'd have his good days and his bad days. Sometimes he wouldn't get out of bed for four days straight, but then he would be lively for two and crash again. It meant he couldn't hold down a job, so Mom had to be the stable one, the one providing, and it also meant she was out working more times than not.

I understood she had to do what she did, but it didn't mean I had to like it. Dad had been gone for almost nine years, so why was she still working the way she used to? She had Sal now. She had support. But that didn't stop her working all the hours she could. Nothing had changed, and yet *everything* had changed.

Maybe it wasn't about the money. Maybe she couldn't stand seeing my dad's eyes every time she looked at me. Maybe staring at my face reminded her of him. My chest started to cave in, my thoughts weighing me down, and I was sure to sink at a moment's notice.

"Hey, sweetheart," Mom's tired voice called as

the door to the kitchen swung open. The bags under her eyes told a story of little sleep, and the way her feet dragged showed me how tired she really was. "How you getting on?"

"Good," I said as I placed another pot in the dishwasher and closed it up. "Is it still busy out there?"

She huffed out a breath and closed her eyes briefly. "Starting to die down now." She gently grasped my arm. "I'm sorry you had to help out."

"It's okay." I flashed her a smile, the same smile I always gave her that held secrets behind it. Secrets I would never reveal to her. "You were busy."

"I hate that you have to do this." She let her head drop back. "As soon as the other diner is up and running, we'll have more time on our hands. Everything will change then."

"Mom." I placed my hand over hers. "It's okay, really. I don't mind."

It wasn't actually working in the diner that bothered me. It was the amount of time the diner took away from Mom and me. Growing up, we'd always been close, but the last couple of years I'd drifted away from her. It was no one's fault, we just…had our own things going on. She thought I was doing fine, and I knew how much she loved opening up her own diner.

But today…today I witnessed the sadness in her eyes. She'd been devastated that day, and she'd managed to hide it from me over the years, but right now it was at the forefront, showing me how much she still hurt.

I couldn't let her see my torment, though. I had to push it down and hide it away. I had to be strong for everyone around me because if I showed them exactly how weak I was, I wasn't sure what would happen.

"How do pizza and a movie sound once I've finished my shift?" Mom asked, the sadness in her eyes turning to hope.

"Sounds good," I replied, a genuine smile on my face this time. It had been too long since it was just the two of us hanging out like we used to. It was always Mom and me against the world, but somewhere along the way that had changed.

"Why don't you head out front and get some homework done, and I'll finish up here for you?" Mom rolled her shoulders, probably trying to wake herself up a little.

"It's okay, I got this, Mom. If we work together, we can get out of here quicker."

"You're right." She pushed some hair that had fallen out of her ponytail behind her ear. "You always were the clever one," she commented as she started to clear away the pots as they came out of the dishwasher. "I feel like I haven't spoken to you properly since you started senior year."

"I know," I murmured. "But it's been going good."

"Yeah?" She grinned wide and held a pan in each hand. "Any boys asked you out yet?"

"Mom." I groaned and rolled my eyes. It was always one of the first things she asked, and I always gave her the same answer. "Of course they haven't."

Mom let her hands drop to her sides. "What do you mean, 'Of course they haven't'?" The heavy pans looked like they were weighing her down, and the apron around her red diner dress was covered in food stains, but it didn't deter her from looking scary as hell.

"Seriously, Mom?"

"What?" She stored the pans away and planted her hands on her hips. "You're my beautiful Aria, they're dumbasses if they don't ask you out."

"So you want me to be going out on dates with horny teenage boys?" I raised a brow and pulled the lid down on the dishwasher for what felt like the hundredth time.

"Well…" She trailed off and looked away from me at the sound of the kitchen door opening.

"What are you two rambling on about in here?" Sal asked, his gruff voice cutting through the silence in the kitchen. His face was covered in a frown, but I knew it was just his *normal* look. Sal was scary look- ing, but those closest to him knew he was a giant teddy bear, one who would do anything for the people he loved.

"Mom is trying to whore me out," I casually stated.

Mom gasped, her hand flying to her chest. "I would never!"

"Mmmmm, don't lie, you want me out of the house and getting drunk at high school parties—"

"No parties," Sal interrupted. "Or boyfriends." He halted next to Mom and pointed in my direction. "Boys are trouble."

"Yes, they are," Mom replied, raising her brow at him. "You being the biggest trouble of them all."

"Me?" Sal pointed his thumb at his chest, his brows high on his forehead. "I'm a goddamn angel, Jan. An angel."

Mom snorted and shook her head. "If you say so."

"I do say so." Sal stepped forward and hooked his arm around Mom's waist to pull her against his chest.

I raised my hand and screwed up my nose. "Ew. Daughter present."

"Tell her she should be out having fun, Sal," Mom pleaded with him.

"Nope. If she was out having fun, what kind of teenager would she be?" Sal flicked his gaze over to me and winked. "That would make her normal."

I pulled open the dishwasher when the two-minute cycle had finished. "You're both so…so…"

"So what?" Mom asked.

"Ugh." I threw my hands up in the air. "You're driving me insane."

"So that's a yes to going out with Hope on Friday then?" Mom asked as her lips spread into a knowing smile. The sneaky…

"Have you been looking at my messages?" I accused, backing away from both of them. I didn't even know why I was surprised by the fact, I'd once found messages from her to Hope trying to arrange a friend date.

"They just happened to come through while I was standing next to your cell." Mom shrugged and wrapped her arms around Sal's waist. "You should go out, have some normal teenage fun."

"I don't want 'teenage fun.'"

This wasn't normal. My mom shouldn't tell me to go out on a Friday night with my best friend, especially when said friend was going to be attending a concert with her older sister and her boyfriend at some bar in town. That meant more than teenage fun. That meant bars and clubs and…

"You should go," Sal said with a clip of his head. "Make sure you're back by curfew."

"I don't even have a curfew." I shook my head and let out a puff of air. "How are you two even parents right now?"

"We're down with the kids." Mom flipped her ponytail. "We're cool."

"Cool?" I let my head drop back and groaned loudly. "If I get kidnapped while I'm out with Hope, it'll be all your fault."

Mom's tinkle of laughter surrounded us. "That's okay, we know some DEA agents. I'm sure they'd try and find you."

———

ARIA

"I'm not sure about this."

I shifted side to side and stared in the mirror at the outfit Hope had chosen for me. The flowy, emerald-green top tied at the back of my neck and showed all of my back, with only a strip around the waist and the front covering me from neck to hips. From the front, it was conservative as hell, but the back was a whole other story.

"I think you look hot as shit." Hope pushed a giant hoop earring through her ear and came to stand behind me. "Those jeans are like a second skin."

I stretched my legs out and cringed at the feel of the tight, faded black denim. I was used to skinny jeans, but these were practically painted on.

"I'm still not sure."

"Stop overthinking, Aria. Just go with the flow." Hope handed me a pair of block-heeled boots.

"I—"

"Girls? You ready?" Hope's sister, Lisha, asked. Her heels clicked on the wood floor in the hallway, and then Hope's bedroom door swung open. "Cab will be here in a few minutes." Lisha's black hair was exactly the same as Hope's, but where Hope hated her pale skin, Lisha embraced it.

"We're nearly ready," Hope replied and turned to stare at me one last time. "You look hot, let's go."

I bit down on my bottom lip and pushed my feet into the boots. They gave me a couple more inches of height which I desperately needed. I windmilled my arms out a couple of times, trying to find my balance, and took one final look in the mirror.

My hair was curled and starting to drop, giving me a wavy look, and my makeup was minimal. I may have caved on the outfit, but there was no way I would let Hope loose on my face. That was a step too far.

This wasn't the first time I'd gone out with Hope and her sister, but the last time hadn't gone too well. We'd ended up carrying Lisha home after an argument with her boyfriend and spent the remainder of the night doing nothing. I just hoped tonight wouldn't be a repeat.

"Come on, Aria!" Hope shouted from somewhere in her apartment.

I took a deep breath, picked up my faded denim jacket, and walked out of her bedroom and into the hallway. Hope's apartment was much like mine with a living room connecting to the kitchen, and a bathroom. The only difference was she had three bedrooms. It was small and compact, but it served them well, just like ours did us.

By the time I got to the front door, I'd gotten used to the block heels a little and felt much more steady.

"You ready for this?" Hope asked, and hooked her arm through mine.

"Not really." Her answer was to laugh, and together, we walked down the couple of flights of stairs and into the lot of her apartment building.

The cab was waiting for us as we exited, and then we were on our way to the bar Lisha's boyfriend was playing at tonight. I knew without Lisha I wouldn't have gotten in, but I had doubts they'd let me in at all. I was only a few months out from my eighteenth birthday, and although I may not have looked my age, I didn't act like it either. I was more than happy staying home and not going out, which was part of the problem. I didn't go out and enjoy myself, I didn't let my hair down. Maybe Mom and Sal were right? Maybe I needed to have some normal teenage fun for once. I was sick and tired of everything weighing on me, so by the time I exited the cab and followed Lisha and Hope into the bar, I resolved to let go.

Let go of the anger I constantly felt rushing through my veins.

Let go of the sadness that weighed me down.

Just…let go.

Lisha headed right for the stage while Hope and I settled at a table. After a few minutes, a tray of shots was placed down in front of us.

"Perks of knowing the band," Hope said, but there was a sadness to her tone. Something had seemed off with her all night, but I hadn't wanted to say anything. She picked up a shot and downed it without a second thought, then passed me one. "Go on."

I inhaled a deep breath, plucked the glass from her hand, and threw back the shot. The cool liquid rolled over my tongue and slid down my throat, leaving a burn in its wake. But the burn told me I was alive. The burn spurred me on for another one, and as Hope was reaching for her second, I did the same.

"That's my girl!" Hope shouted as Lisha sat at the table.

"You started without me?" Lisha asked.

"You snooze you lose." Hope shrugged and picked up two more shots, handing one to me. "We'll get a different drink after this."

I nodded in reply and downed the shot, the

burn now becoming unbearable. "Shit, that one hurt." I groaned and rubbed my chest with the palm of my hand.

Lisha and Hope laughed, but their shots didn't seem to have affected them in the slightest. I wondered if this was what Hope did when she had to go away with her sister? Did she sit beside the stage and drink all night?

Music blasted throughout the room as the band started playing, and Lisha jumped from her seat and onto the dance floor, front and center. "I don't know why she does that," Hope said, her voice louder to be heard over the music. "She's so…desperate."

I turned in my seat and stared at Lisha. Her hands were up in the air, her head thrown back, and from here, it looked like she was having a blast. "She looks like she's having fun." I grinned and faced Hope. "Let's get another drink and go join her."

Hope's eyes widened. "Oh, I see Party-Aria has come out to play."

I stood and pulled off my jacket, relishing in the cool air as it hit my exposed back. "Mom told me to have fun. I'm only doing as I was told."

"Your mom is seriously the best!" Hope hooked her arm over my shoulders and pulled me toward the bar. We both ordered another couple of shots and some water to wash them down afterward. Mom's words about keeping hydrated echoed in my mind over and over again. Although, I wasn't sure she meant it quite like this.

The bass of the music became louder, reaching a crescendo, but it didn't end. Instead, it seamlessly flowed into the next song on their setlist. We weaved our way through the growing crowd at the bar and onto the dance floor where I threw my hands in the air like Lisha had.

All the songs seemed to merge into one. Shots were handed to me from both Lisha and Hope, and I downed them greedily. They said know your limits, but tonight, I was forgoing all of that. I was letting go, dammit, and I was determined to have a good time, even when the band stopped performing and the sound system was all that was left playing music.

"I'm heading backstage to check on Lisha!" Hope shouted, and I nodded in reply, too busy swaying my hips on the dance floor. There were fewer people on it now, but it was still half full of couples and friends all having a good time.

I uncapped my bottle of water and took a swig but came up empty just as a pair of hands gripped my hips from behind. Sober me would have pulled away, but drunk me was having the time of her life, so I swayed my hips in time with the music.

A chest pushed against my back, buttons pressing into the soft skin, and I shivered from the cool contact. The hands traveled around to my stomach and pulled me closer still, and it was then I realized what was digging into my ass.

I tried to pull away, but the hands gripped me tighter as a groan vibrated through my ears.

"Let me go," I tried to say, but it came out a slurred mess. I looked around, seeing all the faces but not recognizing one of them. How long ago had Hope left to go and check on her sister? How long had I been here? I had no concept of time, and it was then I realized what a huge mistake I'd made.

I'd let go of everything when I shouldn't have.

I'd let my guard down, and I'd only ever done that once in my life. The one time I regretted more than anything.

I tried to pull away again, but the guy wouldn't let up. My breaths came faster, and I could hear my blood whooshing in my ears. I needed help. I needed out of here. But I couldn't move. I couldn't get away. This was the reason I never went out. This was why I kept my walls so high no one could climb over them.

I twisted to the side, my gaze flitting around the room, but I couldn't concentrate on any one thing. I'd made a mistake coming here. I'd made a mistake not knowing my limits. I'd fucked up, and now I saw no way out of it.

"Let go," I repeated, this time much clearer. I was gaining my wits, and sobering the hell up. At least I thought I was until the guy let me go and I stumbled forward. My knees hit the ground before I realized what had happened, and it took me a couple of seconds to make the room stop spinning.

I crawled over to the table we'd been sitting at and grabbed my jacket then used the chair to stand up. The restrooms were only a few feet away, so I made for those while trying to fish my cell out of my pocket.

My balance was off thanks to the shots, so I was glad there was a wall I could lean on to guide me down the hallway and to—

"Whoa." Gentle hands gripped my arms. "Sorry."

"That's okay," I slurred out, resting my head against the cool wall. My hair fluttered over my face, and I batted at it, needing to get it out of my eyes.

The hands moved off my arms and were then on my face. "Aria? What the hell?" I'd recognize that gruff voice any day of the week, and I couldn't help but sigh.

"Hey, Cade." My lips pulled up into what I could only assume was a sloppy smile.

"Are you drunk?" His fingertips pressed against my hot cheeks. "Jesus fuckin' Christ, does your mom know you're here?"

I nodded, or at least, tried to, but it was hard with his large paws stopping any movement. I reached up to try and move them off my face, but as soon as my small hands covered his huge ones, I forgot what it was I was trying to do.

"Mom told me to go out and have fun." I finally met his stare in the dim hallway and inhaled a breath. His cologne wrapped around us, and I grinned. There was nothing like the musky smell that seemed to follow Cade around. "I was having fun," I pouted, "until some guy on the dance floor pressed his dick into my ass."

"I…fuck me." Cade groaned and let go of my face, but pulled one of my hands into his. "Come on, I'm taking you home." I didn't answer him as he led me back through the hallway and into the bar area. He walked me near the door and said, "Wait here."

I did as I was told and slumped against the wall, waiting for my knight in shining armor to whisk me away. Or maybe I would sleep. Sleep sounded real good right now.

Chapter Seven

CADE

I didn't want to leave her alone, but I didn't have a choice. She was drunk off her ass, and I was here with some teachers from school, so there was no way I could bring her back to the table we were sitting at and tell them I was taking her home.

Pushing my way through people in the crowded bar seemed like it took an age when, in reality, it was only seconds. I turned back when I was a few feet away from the table where Willow and Harold were sitting, and spotted Aria sliding down the wall. What the hell had she been thinking?

"I've got to head out," I told the table as I grabbed my leather jacket and keys.

"What?" Willow stood and nearly knocked the drinks over as she reached for me. "It's only eleven.

It's still early." Her palm connected with my forearm, her fingers covering the tattoos that were now
on display. I kept them hidden while I was at school
because it was policy.

"I know but"—I flicked my gaze over to the
front door and spotted Aria still there, only now it
looked like she was asleep—"my dad called. He
needs some help." I shrugged her off and backed
away a step. "I had a blast, though. Same time next
week?"

That seemed to placate her because she smiled
and trailed her hand down to her chest. The signs
were all there. If I wanted Willow, I could have her.
But that was the problem: I didn't want her.

A couple of years ago, she would have been my
go-to woman, but now, not so much. I'd learned not
to waste a second of my life, not when it could be
gone within the blink of an eye.

"Definitely," she breathed out.

"I'll see you all at school on Monday." I didn't
wait for any of them to reply as I spun around and
headed back toward Aria. My palm itched to pull
out my cell and call Jan to tell her what had
happened, but something stopped me. I was her age
once not so long ago, and I would have hated the
person who ratted me out.

Aria was more or less lying on the floor by the
time I got back to her, so I crouched down and

placed my hand on her face. "Aria? Come on, you need to get up."

"I'm tired," she groaned, her words coming out slurred. How much had she had to drink?

"I know." I let out a slow breath. "I'll take you home."

"Okay." She reached her arms out, her eyes still closed. "Carry me. I can't get my legs to work."

I shouldn't have wanted to laugh at her. I should have been angry that she'd gotten herself into this state. Livid that she'd come to this bar. Raging that they served her. But I was none of those things, especially when she cracked open her eyes and stared at me. Her light-brown eyes looked almost gold in this light, and they drew me in, threatening not to let me go.

There was always something so intense when Aria stared at me fully. Almost like she was seeing through all my bullshit and staring at the roots that made me who I was.

I shook my head and hooked my arms under her legs and against her back. The silky smooth skin of her back greeted my palm, and my stomach dropped. I shouldn't have pressed my fingers deeper into her skin, I shouldn't have been trying to memorize how soft it was, but I was doing both of those things, and nothing could stop me.

Aria rested her head on my shoulder, her breaths flowing across my neck, and I stumbled a little as I stood. My body shouldn't have been reacting this way to a drunk woman—girl. She was just a girl. She was seventeen, and almost like a sister to me.

But I couldn't deny the way my body buzzed when I was around her. I couldn't deny how much I craved to see her and hear her gentle, calming voice. Maybe it was the couple of beers I'd had? Maybe they'd affected me more than I'd thought. If that was the case, then there was no way I was going to be driving home.

I walked out of the club with Aria pressed against me and held my arm out at the edge of the sidewalk. A cab pulled up not three seconds later, and I pushed us into the back. I had no idea what I was going to do or where I was going to go, but the thought of taking her home and getting her into trouble didn't appeal to me.

I shot off my address to the cab driver, my mind made up. There wasn't any harm in her being there. It was only one night. I'd look after her, make sure she didn't puke her guts up, and then take her home in the morning. My dad had taught me how to treat the people we cared about, and there was no doubt I cared about Aria. She'd been there when I'd gotten shot, and I'd been there the day everything in her life changed.

. . .

"He's gone," she whispered, tears rolling down her face. She was so small—smaller than any other eight-year-old I knew. Her pale skin and bright red hair were such a contrast that it almost looked fake, but no one could deny the absolute heartbreak showcased in her eyes.

"It's okay, Aria." I held my arms open for her, and she came willingly. The waiting room was full of people from all walks of life, but there were only two people we were here for —Aria and her mom.

"I…" She hiccupped a sob and held my T-shirt tighter. I squeezed her against my chest, wishing I could take away every ounce of pain she was feeling in that moment. "I saw him. I…I found him."

My stomach bottomed out. "You found him?" I asked. I had to make sure I heard her right. It was one thing feeling the loss she did, but to have witnessed that trauma was something else entirely.

She nodded against my chest, the sobs getting more gutwrenching and I knew I couldn't let her stay here, not surrounded by people staring at her. Dad and Lola were seeing to Jan who sat staring at a wall, not a single emotion on her face, but Aria…no one was there for Aria, and I promised myself there and then I'd always be there for her, no matter what happened.

The cab slamming on its brakes brought me out of my head and I stared down at Aria. It was the only time I'd seen her cry, because after that day nine years ago, she'd locked it away and become someone completely different. She'd had to push it into a part of her brain she wouldn't access, because if she didn't, she wouldn't be able to live day to day.

I understood her more now than anyone ever would.

Aria stirred in her seat and then snapped her eyes open. "I'm gonna be sick."

"Shit." I flung the door open and helped her out, just in time for her to throw up against the curb. Fishing a few dollars out of my pocket, I then passed them to the cab driver who promptly squealed away from us.

"I'm never drinking again." She groaned and let her head drop forward, then a second later she was throwing up again. I dropped my jacket and hers on the ground and held her hair back. The streetlights illuminated part of the street, but I wasn't sure if I was thankful for the light or wished it wasn't there.

She dry-heaved a couple of times and finally tried to stand. "I need water." I picked our jackets up and wrapped my arm around her waist. "And food. I'm starving."

I chuckled. "Only drunk you'd want food right after you throw up."

"You have such huge hands," Aria commented, her voice breathy, but it was nothing like how Willow had spoken to me. When Willow spoke, it drifted right over my head, but Aria's voice hit me right in the pit of my stomach.

She grabbed hold of my fingers on her waist and trailed her fingertip over my thumb. "Have you ever measured your fingers?"

I raised a brow as I halted us outside my door. "Measured my fingers?" I asked and pushed my key into the lock. She was still leaning against me, and I liked her pressed against my side. She was Aria. The girl who bugged me to no end growing up, but she was also the girl who I would protect with my life.

"Yeah. Like in centimeters."

I pushed the door open and helped her over the step, in case she missed it, and then flicked the lights on. She slammed her hand over her eyes and stumbled back into the wall as I locked the door behind us.

"Jeez, Cade, give a girl some warning."

"Lights are on," I answered her, and grabbed her wrist to lead her into the kitchen.

"Har-har—oh shit, where's my cell?"

"Have you checked your pocket?" I asked and sat her on one of the bar stools. It probably wasn't a good idea to have her sit there while she was intoxicated, but it was the only chairs I had down here. My other downstairs furniture wasn't due to be delivered until tomorrow.

"Ha, found it." I filled up a glass with some tap water and turned around to hand it to her, but in the seconds between her last words, she'd rested her head on the counter and was now snoring up a storm.

I stood and stared at her for several seconds, wondering what had changed about her since I'd left for college seven years ago. She'd been ten at the time, and although I was there for her, I was also too busy hanging with my friends and visiting with my baby sister. I'd forgotten about her somewhere along the way, and I wasn't sure anyone else hadn't either.

She was the quiet girl in the corner. The one you could trust to sit and wait for you for several hours. The one you trusted not to get into trouble. But was that really who she was? It was a Friday night, and I'd found her drunk at the bar.

I wasn't sure I knew the Aria in front of me anymore, but that made me all the more determined to get to know who she was now.

———

ARIA

My tongue was stuck to the roof of my mouth, thanks to the dryness of my throat. That, coupled with the banging inside my brain, told me I was hungover. My stomach rolled at the memory of the shots I'd downed, and I groaned and rolled over. My eyelids cracked open a little and closed back up, and it took me a couple of seconds for them to fling open at what I'd seen.

This wasn't my room.

My room wasn't gray with an open blind. And I certainly didn't have a huge comfortable bed at my disposal. Where in the ever-loving hell was I?

I stayed still, so very still I resembled a statue. My ears perked up, and I heard voices. Several voices I didn't know—voices that made me hyperventilate. I tried to take stock of where I was because I needed an escape plan, one where I could get out of this house without anyone noticing.

Tentatively, I pulled the covers back, thankful all my clothes were still attached to my body. That was a good sign, right?

My cell sat on the nightstand, and I grabbed for it, opening up my messages, about to ask Hope what the hell happened last night. But what I saw had my eyes widening and my brain even more puzzled than it was before.

Hope: Where are you? I've searched the bar, but I can't see you.

Hope: Holy shit. Some teachers are here!

Hope: If you don't answer me, I'm going to call your mom.

Aria: I'm fine. I got a ride home from Sal.
Call you tomorrow.

The grammar and punctuation on my text meant it wasn't me. Who the hell had sent this, and—

"Aria?" My eyes widened at the rough voice, and I nearly squealed when a knock rang on the bedroom door. "You awake?"

Cade? How the hell had I ended up…

Oh, shit.

The memories from the night before were resurfacing and slapping me right in the face. What had I gotten myself into?

"I…I'm awake," I croaked out, my voice sounding nothing like my own. I wasn't sure whether it was because I'd just woken up, or because I'd drunk my weight in alcohol last night.

The door creaked open slowly, and then Cade's face was in view, along with the shorts and tight T-shirt he'd decided to torture me with today. Could a girl not catch a break? I was over here hungover with breath that could rival a skunk, and he was… well, he was Cade.

"How you feeling?"

I gripped my head and flopped back on the bed. Now that I knew whose house I was in, I was no longer in immediate danger. "Like I got run over by a truck." His laugh echoed around us, and I hated him even more for the way my ears loved the sound.

"I'm gonna head out and get some breakfast now that my furniture has been delivered. You can take a shower while I'm gone."

I rolled over and stared at him. *Really* stared at him. He was taller than he had been the last time I'd seen him nearly five years ago, but the Cade I knew was still in there. This was just a more grown-up, muscular version of him.

"I'd like that," I murmured.

He took a step forward, but his gaze didn't move off mine. I wasn't sure what was happening, but I couldn't have been the only one to feel the tension in the air. Goose bumps sprang over my skin the closer he got, and when he handed me one of his T-shirts and some shorts, my breath stalled in my throat.

I reached forward to take them from him, and my fingertips grazed against his. There wasn't an electric shock that happened, not like they talked about in the books. It was more of a fizzle that slowly boiled over, something just starting out but refusing to be ignored.

Neither of us looked away, and I didn't pull my fingers back. Part of me wanted him to let the clothes go and leave the room, and the other part of me wanted him to hook his finger over mine and pull me toward him. But we couldn't do that. We could never do that. Right?

I moved forward and brought my legs off the side of the bed to stand, but still, he didn't back away. Without the boots on, I only came up to the middle of his chest, tiny compared to him, but I kind of loved that. I liked the fact that if he wanted to, he could cocoon me in his arms and—

What the hell was I thinking?

"Thanks," I finally said, and he shook his head at the sound of my voice, almost as if he was bringing himself out of a daze.

"Welcome." He backed up a step. "Shower is in there. Towels are on the rail."

"Got it."

He nodded and exited without saying another word, and I was left standing in the middle of his room, feeling like a fool. I reasoned the only thing that would make me feel better was hot water against my skin and a tube of toothpaste in my mouth. So I did precisely that. I stepped into his newly tiled bathroom—at least I assumed that was why there were still tools in here—and under the huge showerhead.

The water rained down on me like a waterfall, at just the right temperature, and I was debating whether to come here every couple of days just to have a shower. I didn't think twice about washing my hair, not caring if it dried a frizzy mess.

Once I was out of the shower and dressed in Cade's T-shirt and my jeans from last night, I sat on the edge of his bed and took a second. I needed to get all my thoughts in order. It was one thing sleeping in his bed at Uncle Brody and Lola's house, but it was something totally different being in *this* room.

The air smelled like him, and the little knick-knacks dotted on his chest of drawers were calling to me. I wanted to investigate more of his personal space, intrigued by what he liked and didn't like. The front door clicking closed had me jumping off the bed, afraid he could hear my thoughts from downstairs.

"Aria?" Cade shouted.

"Coming!" I grabbed my cell and my top from last night, then walked down the stairs and toward the smell of bacon.

Cade's back was to me as he stood in the kitchen, plating whatever he'd bought. "I hope you still like bacon," he said, not even looking over his shoulder. He could sense I was here, and I wasn't sure why it unnerved me the way it did.

"I do." I walked forward, spotting my jacket hung over the back of one of the barstools.

Cade spun around and placed two plates on the counter, but I didn't miss the way his gaze settled on my chest. His T-shirt was way too big for me, but I'd tied it at my waist. The soft, gray material cocooned my skin, and I couldn't deny that I never wanted to take it off.

"OJ?"

"Please," I answered him, my voice rougher than usual. I wasn't sure whether it was his dark-blue eyes that was causing it or all the alcohol from last night.

He tilted his head at the two plates on the counter, so I stepped forward and pulled myself up onto one of the barstools. I was glad I'd had a shower and found a spare toothbrush because the thought of sitting this close to him unwashed after last night wasn't appealing.

I dug into the bacon and pancakes on my plate, already knowing he'd gotten it from Sal's. I could taste a Sal pancake from a mile away.

"You went to Sal's?" I asked as Cade sat down beside me. There was only a couple of inches of space between us, and I looked down at the gap with a swallow. One move and his thigh would be pressed against mine.

"Yep." He took a swig of his juice. "I didn't tell them you were here, though. I assumed your mom would think you stayed at Hope's."

I was silent for a couple of minutes, working my way through the food and already feeling better for it. "And Hope?"

"I messaged her from your cell." Cade turned

his face to stare at me. "She was blowing up your cell, and you wouldn't wake up."

"Good job I don't have a passcode on it then, huh?"

Cade shrugged. "I'd have guessed it anyway. You're pretty predictable."

"Oh yeah?" I placed my knife and fork on the edge of the plate, not able to eat another bite. "Let's test that theory."

Cade laughed and spun on his stool, causing his legs to sit either side of me. I didn't know whether he was unaware or just didn't care. "Go on then."

I pulled my cell out and clicked on to have a passcode then handed it to him. "Try to crack that —" He handed my cell back to me, having guessed the correct passcode. "How the hell…"

"Your birthday. Easy. Everyone uses their birthday."

"You think you're so clever, huh, Mr. Easton?"

"No *thinking* about it." He winked and stood. "I know I am."

I shook my head, but couldn't stop the laugh bubbling up. "You're incorrigible." I stared at his back as he rinsed off his plate in the sink and placed it into his dishwasher, and then stood to pass him mine.

"Using big words considering you're hungover," he said, his dark-blue eyes twinkling as they met mine.

"Are you not used to such words on a Saturday morning, Mr. Easton?"

He groaned and took my plate from me. "I hate when you call me that."

Leaning against the counter next to him, I crossed my arms over my chest. "That's your name, isn't it?"

He didn't answer me for several seconds. Instead, he kept loading the dishwasher, his large hands moving backward and forward. "Not to you," he finally said, closing the dishwasher door and standing to his full height. "I'm always just Cade to you."

His dark-blue eyes swirled with something… something I was sure I was imagining. "Cade," I breathed out, suddenly aware of how close we were. "I…"

I wasn't sure what I was going to say, but he stepped forward. I had to dip my head back to be able to keep eye contact with him. "Aria," he answered me, but that one word said so much more than merely my name.

I let my arms drop from my chest and pressed my back to the counter. He was erasing any distance between us, and part of me wanted to scream at him to stop, but the other part of me wanted him to never let there be any space ever again. He'd been back in town for a couple of months, and in that time, all my old feelings had resurfaced. But I'd realized what I felt back then was nothing compared to what was starting to swirl inside of me now.

"Why?" Cade asked, but I wasn't sure he was talking to me as he continued, "Why do you make me feel like I'm losing my mind?"

I swallowed at his words, and my body drifted closer to him, already knowing what it wanted. His hand gripped my hip, his fingers whispering to the small portion of skin between my jeans and his T-shirt, and I moaned from the impact. My stomach dipped, and my body begged for more from him.

"I shouldn't…" He trailed off, and my tongue swiped over my bottom lip on instinct as he dipped down, his face so close I could see every speck of green in his otherwise blue eyes. "But I can't stop myself."

Neither of us looked away, the seconds ticking by, and then he pressed his lips against mine. I wasn't sure what to do at first. My body was frozen, my hands shaking. *Cade was kissing me.* His soft lips were against mine, and I… I couldn't move. I couldn't do anything.

He yanked himself away from me and took two giant steps back. "Shit, Aria." He slapped his palm against the counter and pushed his other hand into his hair. "Shit, I'm sorry. I shouldn't have done that."

His chest was heaving, but so was mine.

I'd been frozen, but that didn't mean I didn't know what I wanted.

———

CADE

I'd made a mistake. I'd done something I never should have. I'd crossed a line.

Fuck.

I paced the kitchen, feeling Aria's eyes on me, but I couldn't look at her. I'd taken it too far. I'd been lulled by a false sense of security and forgotten who I was, and I wasn't sure what had tipped me over the edge. Maybe it was having her in my house all alone? Maybe it was because she slept in my bed last night?

Or maybe it was because she looked so goddamn hot in my T-shirt.

"Cade," her soft voice called, but I shook my head and continued to pace. I'd been stupid, so fuckin' stupid.

I pushed my hands into my hair and gripped it so much my scalp burned, but at least with the pain, I gained clarity. I never should have brought her back here last night, I shouldn't have—

"Cade." Her voice was firmer now, but also closer. "Look at me."

I inhaled a deep breath and slowly turned to

face her. She was so much smaller than me, delicate but resilient, and I'd taken advantage. "I'm sorry, Aria," I said, collapsing onto one of the bar stools. I hung my head, unable to look at her. I'd always kept my emotions in check, but she had a way of making me lose myself.

"No," Aria commanded. "I'm sorry." Her small hand pushed through my hair, and she forced my head back. Her light-brown eyes didn't move from mine, demanding all my attention. "I should have been clearer."

"What—"

She pushed herself between my legs, our heads now at the same height. "You took me by surprise."

"I…" I frowned, not sure what she was saying, but then she slammed her lips onto mine. She wasn't gentle like I was. She was forceful, demanding, and fuck if it didn't turn me on.

Her hands drifted to either side of my face, trying to keep me in place, and I let her because, if I took over, I wasn't sure I'd ever be able to stop. But then she swiped her tongue over my lips, and all bets were off. She'd woken the beast, and there was nothing I could do to stop him now.

I wrapped my arms around her waist and yanked her closer to me. Her chest pressed against mine as I dipped my tongue into her mouth and drew a moan from her. I could live the rest of my life off that moan alone, but it wasn't enough. I needed to touch her. I needed to own every inch of her.

"Aria," I murmured, pulling away slightly. My hands whispered up her back and to her neck as I stared into her eyes. "This is—"

"Don't say wrong," she pleaded and let her forehead drop against mine. "Please don't say that."

I swallowed at the emotion in her voice. "Okay," I croaked out. "Let's start over." I pressed my lips to hers, gentle again, and savored every soft touch. I didn't need to rush, in fact, I wanted nothing more than to take my time.

Aria met each of my kisses with one of her own, and before I knew it, our tongues were twirling against each other, and I was standing. It took little effort to pull her up and hold her at my height, and I deposited her on the counter we'd just eaten at.

The tables were turned, and now I was in control.

"You're making me lose my damn mind," I told her, kissing her neck and going lower to her collarbone. She let her head drop back and gripped my waist with her small hands.

"Please," she begged, but I wasn't sure she even knew what she was begging for as I made my way back to her lips.

"You want this?" I asked, pressing my lips against hers and then pulling away.

"Yes." She grabbed each side of my face, her

chest heaving with her heavy breaths. "God, I need this so bad."

I pulled in a stuttering breath and let it back out again. "I'm yours, baby." I rubbed my thumb over the apple of her cheek, loving the blush rising.

"Say that again," she demanded.

"Say what?" I asked, my voice a low whisper.

"Baby." Her nostrils flared as I dipped my finger under the loose collar of my T-shirt covering her chest. "No one has ever called me that."

"Good." I wrapped my arm around her waist and pulled her flush with my body. She circled her legs around my waist and I groaned as my cock pressed between her legs. There was no way she couldn't feel it, and from the way her eyes hooded, she liked it. "Only I get to call you that."

"You're so bossy." She laughed, and I couldn't help but be fascinated by the sound. She was one of a kind, and I wasn't sure anyone would ever come close to the person she was.

"Don't you forget it, baby." I winked and pressed my lips against hers again, not able to resist for a second longer. I'd thought this was wrong, but it wasn't.

Nothing this good could ever be wrong.

Chapter Eight

ARIA

I didn't know what I was thinking when I entered the locker room. No, scratch that, I hadn't been thinking at all.

For the last couple of weeks, I'd been coming in here for track practice, and I'd done it on automatic for today's PE class. But it had been a mistake, one I couldn't turn back on as voices rang out when people entered.

I left my bag on one of the benches and darted into the bathroom stalls so no one would see me. I'd hide until they were all gone and then be a few minutes late onto the field. If Hope were here, I wouldn't have entered the room, but her sister had called the office telling them Hope was sick. Only I knew it was because they had to get on the road to drive to the next state over for another concert.

I kept my back against the stall door and steadied my breathing as the voices got louder and louder. I wasn't sure what they were talking about, but a shout from the hallway had me jumping.

"Girls, get onto the field!" Cade demanded.

Goose bumps spread over my skin at the sound of his voice, and my breath stuttered out of me. I hadn't even seen his face, and he was already affecting me. I knew this wasn't a good thing, but I didn't want to push the feelings aside. I'd felt...alive since last weekend, something I hadn't felt in so long, and there was no way I was going to give it up.

The voices lowered, and footsteps rang out, then it was silent—my cue to get ready and onto the field. I ambled over to the bench I'd left my bag on, but frowned when I couldn't spot it. I was sure I'd left it here. I walked around the locker room, wondering if I'd left it on one of the other benches, but when I came up empty, I realized what a huge mistake I'd made.

I'd thought the room was empty when I came in, but someone must have spotted me. Shit. Now I had no gym clothes. What the hell was I going to do?

My feet carried me on automatic out of the locker room, down the small hallway past Cade's office, and out onto the track and field. Cade was in the middle of the field, and I grinned at the way he was standing. His hands were on his hips, the long-sleeved gym top he wore clinging to every contour of his muscles.

He turned his head, spotting me, and even from this distance, I could see the frown on his face. He looked back at all the other students, said something to them, and then they dispersed. I knew I had to tell him about my clothes, but I didn't want to tell him the truth. I didn't want to tell him they'd been stolen and I knew who the culprit was as she ran by me on the track.

Jasmine.

I still didn't know what the hell her problem was, but she definitely had one.

I inhaled a deep breath and stepped forward as Cade moved across the field and closer to me. His frown got deeper the nearer he got, and when we were a few feet apart, he asked, "Where's your gym clothes?"

It was on the tip of my tongue to tell him Jasmine had probably stolen them, but I didn't want to admit I was having any problems at school. I didn't want to show any kind of weakness, so I said, "I forgot them this morning."

Cade huffed out a breath and scrubbed his hand down his face. "Fuck." He closed his eyes, looking the opposite of the calm and collected person I knew. "You're gonna have to wear the lost-and-found clothes in my office."

"What?" I stumbled back a step. I'd only ever forgotten my clothes once, but the teacher at the time had let me sit on the sidelines. "Are you serious, Cade?" I dipped my head back, sure my face was pale.

Cade stepped closer but glanced around us. "I can't show you special treatment, Aria. I did the same to someone last week. If I let you sit out then…" His gaze clashed with mine. "I can't let them see I'm treating you differently, baby."

I hated this. I hated him.

But not really.

I understood why. I just didn't like it, and it was all because of Jasmine. "Don't baby me," I growled. "You're gonna make me wear those stinky clothes." My breathing was picking up, each inhale getting shorter and shorter. It wasn't about the fact they'd probably not been washed in months, it was because all they probably had were shorts. Something I couldn't wear. I couldn't expose myself like that. I couldn't let anyone—

"Aria." Cade's eyes narrowed on me. "You okay?" He stepped forward, but his momentum had me taking a step back.

"I'm fine," I croaked out, feeling like I was lost. I was floating on the wind, and nothing could stop me.

"Hey, Coach?" Jasmine called as she halted on the track near us. "Why isn't Aria wearing her gym clothes?" She winked at me, and my nostrils flared. It was definitely her, and she wanted to make sure I knew it.

"She's just going to get changed now." Cade spun around. "Finish your lap, Jasmine."

"Yes, Coach," she said in her sickly sweet tone. I wanted to hurt her, but more importantly, I wanted to hurt myself. I was stupid, so goddamn stupid, and now the train was off the tracks, and there was nothing I could do to save it.

My muscles were slow, my body sluggish, but I turned around anyway and headed back into the building. Cade's office door was open, and I spotted the box right away. The fraying cardboard was marked lost and found and sat in the corner all on its own.

Why couldn't he have just let me off this one time? It wasn't like it was that big of a deal. No one would have come to the conclusion we'd kissed and spent time together simply because he let me off on one class. My fingers drifted to my mouth as I remembered his lips pressed against mine. How gentle he could be and then demanding. He'd fractured the wall I'd built around me, but I needed to repair it, especially after today.

I hated he was making me do this, but I didn't have a choice. I could refuse to wear them, but the thought of disappointing him wasn't appealing. I wanted to do as he said. I wanted to be the Aria he remembered. The one who did as she was told —*always*.

My shaky legs carried me toward the box, and I kneeled down in front of it. My last slither of hope was finding something that would cover my legs completely. Something had to be on my side, right?

I rifled through the clothes, tossing half of them into a pile of "no way in hell" and then another into a pile of "that's disgusting" which only left me a choice of two T-shirts and a pair of shorts. Dark-blue shorts that were the kind that stuck to every inch of skin. The T-shirts were huge, but that could work in my favor. It'd allow me to cover what I couldn't with the shorts.

Time was ticking by, but I knew I didn't have long until Cade would be in here demanding me to get outside. So I pretended. I pretended I didn't cover my legs one hundred percent of the time. I made believe I was wearing leggings and not shorts. I acted like the T-shirt was coming to my knees when, in actual fact, it stopped just beneath the shorts that only reached mid-thigh.

I was exposed for all to see, and there was only one person who was to blame: myself. If I hadn't kissed Cade, he would have let me sit out. If I hadn't gone into the locker room, Jasmine wouldn't have stolen my clothes. If I didn't...

My gaze flicked down to my legs as I walked back outside, and my vision blurred at what I saw. I was used to seeing them, but never in the outside daylight. They looked so much worse than they did when I was in my room.

And it was all my fault.

I'd done this to myself.

I'd littered my skin with scars.

It was no one's fault but my own. And all it made me want to do was hide. Hide from all the girls on the field. Hide from Cade, the one person who had always made me feel safe. But most of all, I needed to hide from myself. I wasn't the same innocent person I used to be. I had demons. Demons that captured me and wouldn't let go. And now that demon was out in the open for everyone to see.

"Three laps to warm up, Aria!" Cade shouted from somewhere on the field, and I swallowed. Maybe if I kept to the track for the entire class, no one would see them. I could sit on the sidelines while everyone got changed, and I could hide away from them all. I was used to doing it, so it wouldn't be a problem.

Right?

———

CADE

I hated being so hard on Aria, but I didn't have a choice. I couldn't let anyone think she was getting special treatment. I had to keep up appearances, I just hoped she understood why.

We'd crossed a line. A line I never wanted to go back on. I shouldn't have been standing in the middle of my PE class thinking about the way my skin buzzed when I was near her. I shouldn't have loved the way her honey eyes stared into mine. Eyes that held secrets. Secrets I craved to know.

Girls giggled behind me as they picked their teams, and when I turned around, I witnessed them staring at Aria who was stretching on the track. Part of me wanted to make her come onto the field and take part in the game, but I knew I couldn't. I was giving her special treatment. I was letting her stay on the track because at least the rest of the class had seen she was wearing lost-and-found clothes. I'd made my point, even though I hated it.

The teams got their game underway, but I kept flicking my gaze over to Aria. She was meant to be warming up, but she'd sprinted the two laps and now was halfway to the third. She was going all out, and as someone who used running to get away from my problems, I could see she was angry and upset.

I'd caused that. I'd done that to her.

Fuck.

I should have told her to slow down. I should have stepped in, but I wasn't sure how much good I would do. She was in trapped in her own head, and I needed to let her work it out. I couldn't come to her rescue, no matter how much I wanted to.

A team scored, and I looked away from Aria to the field and then back again, just in time to see her trip over. Her hands came out to save her, but even from this distance, I could see the way her ankle twisted.

Laughing surrounded me, and I zoned in on the loudest. Jasmine hollered at Aria and made a show of getting everyone to join in on the laughter, causing my blood to boil. I narrowed my eyes, wondering if Aria had really forgotten her clothes. From the not-so-subtle whispers coming from Jasmine, I wasn't too sure she had.

"Pack the equipment away," I demanded, my voice coming out razor-sharp. If there was one thing I couldn't stand, it was girls like her. I darted across the field as Aria tried to stand up. "Aria!" I called, but she ignored me and tried to put weight on her leg. She howled in pain and collapsed on the track. "Aria, stop!"

"Leave me alone," she said when I was a few feet away. Her shoulders moved up and down as she tried to catch her breath.

"You were meant to warm up," I told her, crouching down in front of her and gripping her ankle. I tried to ignore the electricity that shot through me at touching her bare skin, but even I had to take a second to get myself under control. I couldn't let anyone see the effect she had on me, not here.

"That's what I was doing, Mr. Easton," she gasped out.

"No," I shook my head and raised a brow as I moved my attention off her ankle and to her face. "You were running on anger."

She bit down on her bottom lip and looked away. I didn't blame her. She was pissed at me, and so she should be. I'd gone too far, pushed too much, done what I always did.

Instead of trying to get her attention, I prodded around her ankle, watching for any signs of a break, thankful when it looked like a sprain.

"I'll think you'll live," I said, pulling my lips up into a smile. She still wouldn't look at me though, so I moved my other hand to her other ankle and encased it in my palm. I needed her attention to be on me, I needed her to look into my eyes and see the apology I was too chicken shit to give her. "Aria?"

She closed her eyes at the sound of her name, her throat bobbed as she swallowed, and then finally, she looked at me. "Yes, Mr. Easton?" It killed me that she'd used that name and not Cade, but it was through no one's fault but my own. I'd told her off. I'd punished her for something she hadn't even done.

"You okay?" I asked, instead of what I should have said. I should have told her I was sorry. I should have told her I was trying to show she didn't mean anything to me. But it was impossible. It had been six days since my lips first touched hers, and no matter what I did, I couldn't stop thinking about it. She'd woken a part of me that had been comatose. She'd breathed life back into me, and she had no idea she'd done that.

"Fine."

That word. It was one word which was never used in a rightful way. No one who was fine ever said they were fine. In fact, it was usually the opposite.

I let my head drop and inhaled a deep breath. I was surrounded by students who were no doubt watching us. I couldn't say what I needed to say to her, which was that I'd fucked up. That things had happened while I was gone which changed me forever. She didn't understand, and I wasn't sure I wanted her to. It was an excuse; one I didn't want to use on her.

My eyes tracked her legs, stopping at her knees, and just as I was about to glance at her face, I noticed something on her inner thigh. It was an inch or so above her knee, but…wait…was that? My hand trailed up her leg on its own accord, my body working on automatic as I stared at her soft skin covered in scars. Old scars, new scars, and even a fresh-looking cut.

I was centimeters away from her knee when her hands slapped down, covering the marks. "Don't," she warned, and only then did I finally look at her face. Her eyes were darker, anger and hatred swirling in their depths, but I wasn't sure if it was directed at herself or me.

"Ar—"

"No." She shuffled back from me and lifted herself up, testing her weight on her leg. She hobbled for a couple of steps but managed to stay upright. "You didn't see anything."

My mind was swirling with thoughts. Thoughts I couldn't get under control. Maybe my eyes had deceived me? Maybe they weren't what I automatically thought they were.

But as I stared up at her, my face level with her hips, I knew my first instinct had been right. Those weren't any kind of scars. Those were self-harming scars, and if the scab was anything to go by, she'd cut herself a few days ago.

How had I not known? How had I been back for a couple of months and not noticed the signs? Did she do it often? Was she...trying to kill herself?

My breath caught in my throat, and I looked up at her. Tears streamed down her face as she stared down at me, so much pain in one look it was almost too much to bear.

"Baby," I croaked out. "What are you doing to yourself?"

She shook her head and swiped her arm over her face. "I…" She moved back a step just as the bell rang out, but I didn't take my eyes off her. Not when she turned, and not when she hobbled all the way back to the building. I tried to put all the pieces together, but they wouldn't fit. This wasn't the Aria I knew. This wasn't the same happy-go-lucky girl who used to bug the shit out of me.

This was a new Aria, one who was riddled with darkness.

Chapter Nine

ARIA

My heart beat wildly in my chest. The thrumming of my pulse echoed in my ears. But I didn't look away from my inner thighs. Only a couple of scars marked the tender skin. Two on the left and one on the right. I was trying to even them out, at least, that was what I was telling myself anyway.

The truth was I was starting to crave the pain that accompanied the slice of the sharp blade. I needed to stare at the blood as it trickled out of a cut I'd made. I needed the high it gave me.

I inhaled a deep breath and placed the razor against my thigh, pressing down just enough to cause a pinching sensation. I was only seconds away from breaking the skin, able to bask in the euphoria it would give me, and then I'd feel better than I had since the last time I did it.

"Aria? I'm heading to the——" The bathroom door flung open and my head whipped up.

"Mom!" I wasn't fast enough to conceal what I was doing, and I knew as soon as her gaze lowered down to my shaking hand curled around the blade that she saw what I was doing.

"What...I..." Her sad eyes met mine, her brows lowering as she stepped fully inside the compact bathroom. "What are you doing?"

"I..." I bit down on my bottom lip, preparing to lie, but...I couldn't. Part of me wondered if I'd started doing this to gain her attention, but deep down, I knew it was way more than that. I needed the pain to center myself.

"I'm sorry, Mom." I stood on shaky legs and let the razor drop from my hand and into the sink. The clang of the metal hitting the porcelain rang out around us. "I won't do it again." I clasped my hands together in front of me. "I...I promise."

Mom was perfectly still, the only movement her throat bobbing as she swallowed. I braced myself for the impact that was sure to come. She wouldn't let this slip by, especially not after what happened with——

"Okay," she whispered and stepped back. "You promise?"

I nodded. She was moving farther away, fleeing from the truth showcased in front of her. "I'm..." She cleared her throat and shook her head. "I'm heading to the store; do you need anything?"

"No," I croaked out, staring at her as she bobbed her

head several times and then spun around. Her footsteps echoed down the hallway as she walked away. The sound of the apartment door closing had my body jarring, and I flicked my gaze down to the sink and to the razor.

Maybe I'd do it one last time. Just once, and then I could stop, right?

Five—was the number of years it had been since I made the first cut.

One—was the number of people who knew what I'd done to my body.

Three—was the years it had been since my mom thought I'd stopped.

I'd been keeping a secret from everyone. No one would understand why I needed to do it. They didn't understand it wasn't about anything but feeling the relief and—for one second—not being me.

I was a pro at making myself look put together. I could fool the one person who knew me better than anyone. Sure, Mom still had concerns, but she had no idea what I did when I shut my bedroom door. It wasn't like she was home most of the time anyway. She was too busy working double shifts and looking over the plans to the new diner. She didn't see it because she wasn't looking. She ignored the signs, and that was more than okay with me.

Just like she ignored the fact it was Friday and school had finished ten minutes ago.

My ankle was sore and pulsating. I needed ice and to rest it, but I couldn't do that until I was home. There was no way I'd attempt walking, which meant I had to wait until she turned up.

"Need a ride?"

My shoulders slumped at the sound of his deep voice, and my hands started to shake. At this point, he was my only option, but I was afraid.

Afraid of what he'd say.

Afraid of who he'd tell.

Afraid of being in a confined space with him after what he'd seen.

"I'm good," I said, trying to make my tone sound light and airy, but it was anything but that. My words were broken, much like my soul.

I heard his huff a second before he sat next to me on the step. His long legs stretched twice as far as mine did, and his sleeves were now pushed up, showing his tattoos. I hated that my gaze veered over to him. I didn't want to look at him. But there was nothing I could do to stop it.

He knew my secret. He witnessed the darkest part of me. And the worst thing was, I couldn't take it back.

"Aria." My name rolled off his tongue like he'd said it a thousand times. "You hurt your ankle, and your mom isn't here. Let me give you a ride."

"Mom said she's on her way," I told him. It was a lie, but—

"No, she's not." He held his cell up, and I caught the tail-end of a message. "She messaged me asking if I'd give you a ride."

Shit.

I swallowed and tried to keep my emotions at bay. I was sure I'd see pity in Cade's eyes, and I wasn't willing to let myself see that—not from him. So instead of giving him any eye contact or answering him, I stood and hobbled a couple of steps.

"Let me help—"

"I got it," I told him, wincing when more of my weight landed on my bad ankle. "Motherfuc—"

"You got a potty mouth on you, Aria." His tone was light and teasing, making me forget about everything that had happened today.

It was the thing I was best at: forgetting. Forgetting who I was and what I'd witnessed in my life. Forgetting what I did to myself and forgetting what mattered.

I could feel his hand at my back, and I craved to be able to turn around and collapse into his arms. I needed his safety more than he would ever know, but I couldn't let myself have it. I couldn't rely on him to make me feel okay, not after what he'd witnessed.

We finally made it to his car, and he opened up

the passenger door. He didn't move as I tried to shuffle myself onto the seat. I wobbled, and his hand grasped my waist to right me, and yet, I still didn't look up. I kept my focus on the floor and then on the inside of his windshield when he shut the door behind me.

The engine roared to life a few seconds later, and we were pulling out of the lot and heading toward my apartment. It would only be minutes until I was away from him. Minutes until I was alone again. Seconds until I didn't have to see him for at least two days because I had every intention of hiding from him.

I was so focused on my own thoughts that I didn't realize we'd passed my apartment until it was too late. I looked over at him, careful not to gaze at his face, and watched the way his large hand gripped the steering wheel. "What are you doing?" I asked, my voice low. I was afraid if I talked too loud, he'd come right out and ask me what I was doing— why I was hurting myself.

"I'm hungry. Are you hungry?"

"No."

"More for me then."

I hated how easygoing he was. He was acting like he hadn't seen every exposed piece of me. He was pretending this was any other normal day.

But it wasn't.

He parked outside a burger joint and pushed out of the car, leaving me alone and debating whether I could hobble to my apartment. I rolled my ankle and let out a little squeal. Definitely couldn't make it there.

A few minutes later, Cade jumped back into the car with drinks and a couple of bags in hand and passed them to me. He didn't say another word as he drove out of the lot and back the way we'd just come. But it wasn't my apartment he pulled up at. It was his house.

I should have known he'd bring me here. I should have known he wouldn't let this slide. I should have known because Cade wasn't one to forget things. He wasn't an expert at it like me.

"Cade," I huffed out when he turned the engine off in the driveway. "Please take me home."

"No can do." He took the bags from me. "I'm too hungry to wait." He left me in the car while he carried the bags and drinks inside, but I didn't make a move to get out. I'd stay here until he took me home because the thought of being alone with him and what he would inevitably ask wasn't—

The door flung open, and then I was airborne, my head upside down and my stomach pushing into a shoulder. "What the hell are you doing?"

"Taking you inside."

"Cade, stop! Let me down."

He didn't adhere to my demands. He kept on walking and entered his house. The light walls came into view, and no matter how much I tried to deny it, being back in his space calmed me.

Cade walked down the hallway and finally let me down in the kitchen. The tiles were a mixture of white and gray—glossy and sparkling—and the smell of the food drifted from the counter we'd sat at last week. The same counter he'd placed me on and kissed me.

"I need to go home," I said, but didn't look at him. I kept my gaze focused on the drinks. "I need to take a shower."

"You can take one here," he told me, moving across the kitchen and then pulling the food out of the bags. "After you eat."

"No." I shook my head, and every thought in my brain screamed at me to turn around and head right back out of his door, but something kept me in place. Something overruled my brain and glued my feet to the floor.

I felt rather than saw him move closer, and when his feet came into view, I still ignored him, up until the point his thumb and finger grasped my chin, and he turned my face. "Stop hiding."

"What?" I rolled my eyes. "I'm not hiding. I'm standing right here."

"You won't even look at me."

He had a point.

I looked at him. I finally stared into his eyes and braced myself for what I'd see. But…it wasn't there. The disgust I was sure I'd find shining in his dark-blue eyes was absent, and instead, I found…*understanding?*

The air swirled around us as I waited. Waited for him to ask about the scars littering my inner thighs. Waited for him to ask why I did it. Waited…

"Eat," he said, his voice deeper now, but he didn't let go of my chin. "Eat and then shower."

I opened my mouth, not sure what I was going to say. If I stayed, he'd want answers, and I didn't want him to confront me. I didn't want him to ask any questions. But maybe it was time? Maybe it was time for me to confess my sins and rid myself of the burden on my shoulders? And maybe…

Maybe Cade was meant to be the person I did that with.

His gaze didn't move off mine, his hand stretching to cover the side of my neck as he dipped down and pressed his forehead to mine. "I've got you, Aria." He pulled in a breath and lowered his voice to repeat, "I've got you."

My shoulders slumped.

He was determined to eradicate the wall I'd erected to keep everyone out, and I hated to admit he was getting through it. He was taking it down piece by piece, and there was nothing I could do to stop him.

———

CADE

I didn't know what to do with myself. I paced the length of the kitchen and into the hallway more times than I could count and stopped at the bottom of the stairs several times. My body itched to move up the steps, but I tried my hardest to keep my feet planted on the floor.

She needed space and a little time.

I understood that more than anyone, but it didn't make it any easier. I craved to hold her tight and ask her why. Why was she doing this to herself? Why didn't she think she could talk to anyone? Just…why?

Her footsteps echoed above me, and I wanted nothing more than to help her down the stairs, but she'd refused to let me assist her up them, preferring to hobble slowly, so I waited patiently in the kitchen, listening as her feet met each step. Finally, she appeared and the sad smile on her face had me moving forward.

"You okay?" I asked. It was a stupid question, one that she'd no doubt say yes to, but I hoped she'd tell me no, and I hoped she'd be honest with me. I wished...

I wished she wasn't hurting herself.

I'd kept my words inside as she ate the food I'd bought her and then headed upstairs for a shower. I'd managed to keep myself from going up there, but the more time that passed, the more questions I had.

"Yes," she whispered, in that small, soft voice which always managed to calm me. Even when she was a little girl, she had an aura about her that drew me in. "No," she finally admitted with a slump of her shoulders.

"Aria?" I didn't know why I was trying to get her attention. Maybe it was because I needed her eyes focused on me, or maybe I was trying to portray something to her that even I didn't know.

She stared at the floor, not willing to look up, so I stepped forward and grasped her chin with my thumb and finger, just like I had an hour ago in this very spot. Her soft skin whispered over my fingertips, and I knew right then I wouldn't be able to let her go. I'd opened up a door that had been firmly locked, and now I couldn't close it, no matter what I did.

I didn't want to close it.

Her head tilted back, and she finally gave me her eyes. Honey-colored eyes that kept me captive.

"I…" I had no idea what to say. I didn't know what to ask. I didn't know where to start.

The scars.

Scars I had seen with my own two eyes.

Scars I couldn't ignore.

Scars I hadn't asked her about.

It was my obligation as her teacher to report it, but I knew I wouldn't. I'd bend the rules for Aria. I'd break them. I'd decimate them. Because none of it mattered when it came to her.

"It's relief," Aria blurted out, her eyes misting with tears. "I do it so I feel like I can breathe again."

I swallowed against the lump building in my throat and shuffled closer to her, ready to catch her if she needed me to. "So it's not…" I couldn't say the words. I couldn't form them and get them past my lips. But I needed to know if she was suicidal. I needed to know she wasn't trying to eradicate herself.

"No." She stared at me with sheer determination. "It's never been about that." Her nostrils flared, and she reached up to hold on to my forearm. "You should know that without even asking."

"Should I, though?" I raised a brow, meeting her fierceness with my own. "You're cutting yourself, Aria. You're scarring your skin just to feel relief."

She backed away so fast I swayed forward. "You don't get it." She limped back and forth in front of me. "No one ever gets it."

I frowned and ground my teeth together. "Are you saying other people know you do this?" My anger was boiling over. If people knew, then why the hell was she still doing it? I saw the fresh cut, I witnessed the scab that wasn't years old. I saw the old ones; I saw the amount. God, she had so many, and I was sure there would be more farther up her thighs. She was riddling herself with marks, and it broke my goddamn heart.

She was in a world of her own as she spoke. "Mom found out once"—she laughed, the sound eerie—"but I told her I wouldn't do it again, and she believed me." She dropped her chin to her chest and whispered, "Of course she believed me. Why wouldn't she?"

"Aria…" I wanted to step forward, but I wasn't sure what the right thing to do was. Did she need space? Did she need me to hold her? I had no idea because I'd never been confronted with anything like this before.

"I'm not trying to kill myself," she suddenly said, her voice brooking no room for argument. "I'm not like *him*."

I blinked, not expecting her to have said that. The last time she'd mentioned him to me had been at the hospital nine years ago, and since then, she'd burrowed herself away in her own little safe space. But maybe that was the problem. She hadn't dealt with it, and now it had manifested into…this.

"I can get you help," I told her, straightening my back. "We can make you better, and—"

"Better?" She screwed up her nose. "That's what this is about?" She shook her head, and I heard her huff of breath as she limped toward the door and into the hallway. "I knew I shouldn't have stayed—"

"Stop."

She didn't stop. She kept backing away. She was running from her problems, but I wasn't going to stand here and allow her to do that anymore. She needed to face it head-on.

"Just…leave me alone." She was saying the words she thought she should, but I could hear the sadness behind them. I could sense the heartbreak, but also the silent plea showcased in her eyes. She'd made sure to tell me her mom had believed her, but she shouldn't have. Just because someone said something didn't mean it was the truth.

I darted forward, catching her up in two strides. "No." I grasped her arm and pulled her to me, my arms ready and primed to hold her against my chest. This wasn't me talking to a student. It wasn't even me talking to someone who had become part of the family over the years. This was simply a guy hoping he could help save the girl, even if it was from herself.

"If you don't want to talk to a shrink, then don't."

I flattened my palm against the bottom of her back and dipped down so our faces were level. "If you don't want to put everything out there, then don't." I moved my other hand to the side of her face. "I won't make you promise to not do it again. I won't tell anyone. I won't make you do anything." I paused, hoping the truth shining in my eyes drove my point home. "But I ask that you come to me." I pulled in a breath. "I ask when you feel sad, you come to me. When you feel like you have no other option but to cut, talk to me. If you do cut, reach for me."

"But——"

"No buts." I leaned closer to her. "No ifs, no maybes, just this. You come to me, and I'll always be there, no matter what."

Her gaze flicked between my eyes, searching for the truth behind my words. "Promise?"

"I promise." I pressed my lips gently to hers, sealing it with a kiss. I'd move the earth for her if I could. I probably should have been scared of where my thoughts were going, but I couldn't lose her. I'd only just got her, and I wasn't sure what I would do if something happened to her. She was teetering on the edge of a cliff, but my hand would always be there to pull her back.

I stared at her face as she swiped the tears running down her cheeks. I'd swallow every ounce of her pain. I'd take it all away from her.

"What now?" she asked, her voice cracking with emotion.

"What do you want to do?"

"Sleep."

I pulled my lips up into a smile. "Then, you sleep." I moved my hand off her face and grasped her palm, then led her upstairs. I'd blurred the lines last week, but now I was erasing them, and I couldn't bring myself to regret it one bit.

Chapter Ten

ARIA

I wasn't sure what would happen when we were back at school, not after the weekend we'd had. I'd fallen asleep in Cade's arms and woken up on Saturday morning in the same position. He hadn't asked me about my scars again. He hadn't pried me for more information, and I was thankful for that because I wasn't sure how much more I could tell him.

He'd asked me to come to him when I was struggling, but I wasn't sure if I could. I didn't need him to be the hero. I didn't need him to come to my rescue, but the thought of him being there if I did need him had me at ease.

I may have still been keeping a secret, but someone else knew now, and they weren't trying to lock me away in a mental hospital. They weren't making me go and see a shrink or attend a group meeting. Cade promised to just...be there, which was more than anyone had ever promised me.

"I swear I could sleep for a week," Hope groaned out from beside me. I hadn't seen her much since we'd gone out to see her sister's boyfriend's band. She was spending more days out on the road than in school, and I had no doubt she was falling behind on her schoolwork because of it.

"Rough weekend?" I asked, wincing at the twinge in my ankle with each step I took. I'd rested it most of Saturday after Cade dropped me home, and not moved much at all yesterday apart from getting fresh ice from the refrigerator.

"You could say that." She halted next to my locker and yawned big and loud. "Thank god we only have one class left today. As soon as I get home, I'm crashing."

I opened up my locker and tried my hardest to ignore Jasmine, who was on the other side of me. Normally, her words would puncture me, but today, nothing could touch me. I was floating on a cloud no one could see.

"Aria? Did you hear me?"

"Huh?" I whipped my head around to face Hope and frowned at her. "What did you say?"

"I asked if you had track practice today?"

"Oh." I closed my locker and stepped away

from it. "I hurt my ankle on Friday, so I'm only going to watch."

"That sounds like so much fun," Hope said, her voice monotone. She hated any kind of sport. "I'm gonna head to class." She yawned a final time. "Catch you in the morning?"

"Yep." She twirled around and pushed through the crowd as I shouted, "Get some sleep, you look like a zombie!" She flicked her middle finger up at me, and I laughed as I headed to my last class of the day.

Class trailed by at a snail's pace, but I was sure it was because I couldn't wait to get out of there. I'd never tracked down the minutes until the day ended. I'd never looked forward to what would happen when the final bell rang, but today was different. I may not have been able to practice on the track today, but I could watch by the sidelines and wait...

Wait for everyone to leave.

Wait for Cade to pack everything away.

Wait for Cade to touch me.

Wait for Cade to kiss me.

By the time I made it to the bleachers and sat on them, Reagan and Cade were talking at the side of the track. I couldn't help but watch him as he bent down to show her what her starting position should be.

I tilted my head to the side as his sweatpants

pulled against his ass, and his long-sleeve thermal rode up on his wrists and showed some of his tattoos. His head bent down a little, causing his hair to flop forward onto his forehead, and my fingers itched to be able to swipe it out of his eyes.

Nothing I did could stop me staring at him. Not even the notebook on my lap and the chemistry workbook open next to me. I was enthralled with each of his movements. Obsessed with the way he strode away from Reagan as she got into her starting position.

His head turned left and right, a frown forming on his face until he spotted me. My breath stalled in my chest as his gaze landed on me and froze me to the spot. He was affecting me more than I ever thought possible. My head told me this wasn't going to end well, but my heart didn't care one bit. Not when he was staring at me like I was the only girl in the universe.

He pushed one hand into the pocket of his sweatpants and leaned against the metal rail that encased the track and field. His stare should have been on Reagan and the way she was running, but I was bathing in it instead.

My stomach dipped, butterflies flapping their wings and flying around at a crazy pace. I didn't know how long we stared at each other from so far away, but when Reagan stopped in front of him with her hands on her hips, I finally managed to look away.

I'd never been so captivated by a single person in my entire life. He was consuming my every thought, and there was nothing I could do to stop it —not that I wanted to.

Looking back down at my notebook, I knew I wouldn't get any work done out here, so I packed it away and stood. My ankle was still a little tender, but not enough that I couldn't walk. I didn't want to run on it just yet, but I'd be running at the next practice on Wednesday.

I took the steps slowly, still aware of Cade out of my peripheral vision. He'd moved around the track some, so it meant I didn't have to walk by him to go back inside. But as I made it to the door, I took one glance back. His eyes were focused on me as he took a step toward me. There was still thirty minutes left of Reagan's practice, but I wished there wasn't. I'd never wanted to feel his touch so much before, and I wasn't sure I could wait any longer.

With one deep breath, I turned away from him and entered the building. I was in a daze, but I knew exactly where I was going. The small hallway led to the locker rooms and Cade's office, and I headed right for his door.

It wasn't a big room, but it was enough for what he needed. His desk sat in the middle of the room with two bookcases full of trophies on one wall and a white-board with chairs underneath on the other. Windows made up the other two walls—one set looked out into the hallway, but the blinds on those were closed, and the other set looked out onto the track and field.

I dropped my bag onto one of the chairs and ambled over to the windows, but when I looked out of them, I couldn't see Reagan or Cade on the track anymore. My brows pulled down into a frown as I placed my hand on the glass and narrowed my eyes.

"What are you looking for?" Cade's rough voice asked in a whisper from right behind me. I jumped, but his front pressing against my back kept me in place.

"I—" He moved my hair off my neck and trailed the tip of his finger along the sensitive skin, eliciting a shiver from me. "You…I was looking for you."

"That right?" he asked, his breath fanning over where he'd just touched. I stuttered a breath as his lips met my skin. "God, you drive me insane." I couldn't form any words as he trailed his lips farther down my neck and pulled the strap to my tank top lower. "It took every ounce of strength not to dart across that field and touch you."

I groaned and closed my eyes. Each one of his caresses was simultaneously breaking me apart and putting me back together again. He'd never know how he made me feel. He'd never understand how much I craved his touch.

"Cade," I whispered. His arm wrapped around my waist, his hand flattening on my stomach. I stared down at his long fingers that practically spanned the width of my hips.

"Yeah, baby?" he asked, then flicked his tongue on my neck and followed it up with a kiss.

"Shouldn't you be…" I trailed off as he pulled me tighter against him. There was no denying how turned on he was, and I loved every second of it. I was greedy and wanted more. More of this. More of him. "Shouldn't you be with Reagan?"

He turned me around and pressed his front to mine, keeping me locked between him and the window. "I couldn't stop myself," he told me, his eyes shining with determination. "Not knowing you'd be in here waiting for me."

I whispered my hand up his arm and grasped the side of his neck. "Has she gone?"

His head dipped, and he rested his forehead against mine. "She's gone."

I pulled in a deep breath. "Good." My lips connected with his, but he was ready for me this time. He bent down and picked me up, and I held on to him like he was my life raft.

My legs locked around his waist on instinct as he dipped his tongue between my lips. He stumbled slightly as he maneuvered us across the room and to his desk chair. My thighs sat on either side of him, my hips aligned with his.

"Will I ever get enough of you?" he asked, but I wasn't sure he wanted an answer, so I didn't give him one. Instead, I slammed my lips down onto his and rocked my hips. His erection pushed between my legs, and in response, he growled. "Fuck, Aria." His large hands cupped either side of my neck. "Do that again."

I did as I was told and rocked my hips again. His reaction was nothing compared to the way he rubbed in just the right way. I was losing myself to him, and I didn't care one bit. I forgot where I was. I forgot who we were. I forgot all the pain I felt. The only thing I could think about was the way his lips felt against mine. The way his hands grasped me like I was his, and only his.

Our lips separated slowly, not wanting to be apart, and I finally came up for air. "What are we doing?" I asked him in a whisper.

His eyes were the darkest blue I'd ever seen as his stare captured mine. "I don't know, baby, but I don't want to stop." His thumb rubbed back and forth against the front of my neck.

I smiled, a real smile I hadn't shown anyone for years. In fact, I had a feeling he was the last person who had drawn the smile from me. "I don't either."

Cade closed his eyes, his chest moving on a deep

inhale. "We can't tell anyone, Aria." He pulled me even closer to him. "I hate it, but…"

"I know." I pushed my hand through his hair, relishing in the softness against my fingers. "I get it. It can be another one of our secrets."

His eyes flashed and dipped between us. I knew he was looking at where my scars were beneath the denim of my jeans. When I looked down, I saw the outline of his erection, pointing right at me, and thrust my hips to distract him.

"Fuck, baby." He groaned at the sensation and gripped me tighter. "That feels so goddamn good." He pushed his face into the side of my neck, each of his breaths fanning across my skin and causing goose bumps to rise. "We gotta stop."

"Why?" I asked, loving the way I made him feel. He was exposing part of himself to me, exactly like I had last week, only his wasn't pain-filled like mine.

"Because if we don't…" He didn't finish what he was saying as he pulled back, but the look shining in his eyes told me enough. He was on the verge of losing control, and however much I craved it right now, it was too soon. Everything was weaving together, tightening and threatening not to let us go. One wrong move, and it would all snap. We needed to learn to walk before we tried to run, so I shuffled off his lap and stood in front of him.

"Okay," I said, waving my hand in front of my face to try and calm the blush on my cheeks.

Cade leaned back in his chair, his finger rubbing along his bottom lip as he tracked me from head to toe. "You're something else, Aria Sayer." His gaze finally landed on my eyes. "You know that?" I soaked in each of his words. "I'm not sure whether this is epically stupid, or the best decision I ever made"—he stood slowly—"but I'm not willing to give you up. Not now."

"Is that a promise?" I asked, my voice sounding unsure.

"You're damn straight it is, baby." He threw his arm over my shoulders. "Now come on, I'll take you home so you can do your homework. I hear your world history teacher is a demanding asshole."

I picked up my bag on the way out of his office and grinned up at him. "You heard right."

———

ARIA

If I thought kissing Cade would mean he'd go easy on me in my next practice, then I was wrong. So very wrong. He put me through my paces harder than any other practice. Reagan was off doing her five laps, trying to beat Monday's time, but he kept getting me to do my start position over and over again.

I'd lost count of the number of times I'd bent

down and he'd blown the whistle for me to take off. "Again," he demanded, and I nearly told him to go swivel. My thighs burned, my back ached, and my fingers had imprints from where the track dug into them.

I swiped my hand across my face, bent down, and gritted my teeth at the burn in my thighs. My breaths evened out as I waited for him to blow the whistle, but after several seconds of nothing, I turned my head to face him.

His gaze was focused on me, more specifically, my ass covered by the athletic leggings I was wearing. I raised a brow and cleared my throat, causing his stare to ping to mine. "You about done ogling, Mr. Easton?"

His nostrils flared, and he widened his stance. "What if I'm not?" He paused and flicked his gaze over to the other side of the track.

"Blow the whistle," I demanded, but my voice didn't come out how I meant for it to. It was breathy, a clear sign I liked him staring at me. The last time we'd touched had been in his office two days ago, and it was killing me to be this close to him and not do what I desperately wanted to.

His long fingers reached for the whistle around his neck, and my stomach dipped when I remembered how they'd felt grasping my hips. I could still feel the burn of his palms all over me, and I never wanted it to go away.

"When you take off this time, keep running. Do two laps."

I nodded, but I didn't take my eyes off him. I drank my fill of him in the same way he had done to me. He blew the whistle, and I took off. My start was the best one of the day. I could feel it in the way my muscles extended with each stride. I could sense it in the way my feet hit the track and bounced back up again. Each stride was more confident, taking me around the track faster than I ever had before. It gave me the escape I desperately needed. Cade was a distraction when I was with him, but when I was alone in my bedroom at night, I felt the pain I pushed down during the day.

Cade had asked me to reach out to him, but last night I hadn't. I hated to admit I didn't have the strength to call him up and tell him I was struggling, so instead, I did what I always did. I found relief in the only way I knew how.

But now it was eating at me. I'd not kept my promise. I'd betrayed him, and it made me feel even worse than I already did. By the time I finished my two laps, Reagan was heading into the building, and Cade was waiting by the door.

I slowed down to a walk as I caught my breath, but my thoughts had rendered me speechless. "That was your best time yet," he said, following me through the door. "Well done, Aria."

"Thanks," I whispered, knowing he'd hear me

in the otherwise silent building. The flirtatious banter disappeared because I couldn't even look at him as I walked down the hallway and past his office then into the locker rooms, nearly running right into Reagan. "Sorry."

"It's all good," she said, and I stared up at her. She was a sweaty mess, much like I was. "I saw your last start. It was awesome

A smile quirked on my lips. "Thanks." She'd been running track for years, so she had experience I didn't have. "You have any tips for me?"

She tilted her head to the side and chewed on her bottom lip. "You need to work on your arms."

"My arms?"

"Yeah." She pulled the strap of her bag higher on her shoulders. "I'll show you next practice." Her cell beeped in her hand, and she looked down at it. "My dad is here, I better go."

I nodded. "See you tomorrow."

She didn't reply as she left, and then I was all alone, bar my thoughts. I grabbed my bag out of the locker and pulled out my wash supplies then headed into the showers. There was no way I could put my clothes back on while sweat was still pouring out of me.

I took a quick shower, then wrapped a towel around my body, and sat on one of the benches. My gaze zoned in on the fresh cut on my left thigh, and I couldn't help but drag the pads of my fingers over all the other scars. Some were bigger than others. Some deeper, some more shallow. Some looked angry, some were delicate, but they all represented the agony I had deep down in my heart.

I didn't know how long I sat on the bench and stared at them, but it was a knock on the locker room door that had me jumping out of my skin and covering them up.

"Aria?" A pause and then, "Need me to give you a ride home?"

"I…" I cleared my throat to shout louder. "I need a ride to the diner."

I held on tighter to my towel, afraid he'd come in any second. I knew I needed to tell him what I'd done last night, but I wished I didn't have to. I was trying to appear strong and confident because I didn't want to be the weak one—the one everyone walked on eggshells around.

"Sure. I'll wait out here."

The idea of him only on the other side of the door had me yanking my underwear and clothes on. My light-blue jeans with rips in the knees covered the scars he knew about, and the dark-purple band T-shirt covered my splintered heart.

Once I pushed my feet into my boots, I grabbed my bag and slung it over my shoulder. Cade was leaning against the wall, and as soon as he saw me, he straightened.

I didn't say a word to him as we exited the

building and he locked up behind us. We walked around the outside of it and into the parking lot. Only his car and a couple more taking up spaces. The lights on the black shiny sports car flashed when we got closer, and I opened up the passenger side door and entered his car.

The clean leather smell calmed me, but my pulse quickened when Cade got in and started the engine. My nerves were going haywire at being in such close quarters with him, but I wasn't really sure it was because of that. It was the secret I was holding on to. The broken promise.

Cade pulled up to a stoplight, and I could feel the burn of his gaze on the side of my face. We were only a couple of minutes away from the diner now, and I knew I had to tell him before we got there. It was now or never, and—

"I cut last night," I blurted out. I kept my gaze focused on my hands in my lap, too scared to look up at his face. I wasn't sure what he was going to say, but his silence was a surprise.

The seconds ticked by, each one feeling longer than the last, and then he stopped the car. I looked up, seeing he'd parked right at the back of the lot of the diner.

"Why didn't you call me?" his rough voice asked. When I didn't answer him, he slapped his palm on his steering wheel and repeated, "Why didn't you call me, Aria?"

"I…I…erm…" I gripped on to my hands so tight my knuckles were turning white.

"Aria." His hand landed over both of mine, covering them entirely. "Look at me."

I swallowed and took a deep breath, preparing myself. I glanced up at him and witnessed the torment shadowing his own eyes. "I was scared," I whispered, hating that my throat was closing up. "I…I hate being this person." I closed my eyes and leaned the back of my head against my seat as a lump built in my throat. "This isn't who I was meant to be."

"Baby." His hand moved off mine. I heard a click, and then my belt trailed across my body. "Come here."

I opened up my eyes just in time to see him pushing his seat back, and then he reached for me. I shouldn't have gone to him. I shouldn't have let him take my sorrow away, but the draw to him was too much to deny.

"I'm sorry," I whispered and swiped away a tear from my face. His hands gripped my waist as he pulled me over the center console and into his lap. The safety of his arms couldn't be denied, and I burrowed into his chest, letting him hold me.

"Don't be," he murmured and planted a kiss on the top of my head. "You told me. That's all that matters."

I nodded, but I wasn't sure I agreed with him. I

hated being the person I was. I itched to get out of my own skin. "It was just…it's…" I felt like I needed to explain it to him. Maybe if he understood why, it would be easier. But that was the problem. No one would ever understand why I was the way I was. I'd seen things I shouldn't have. I'd witnessed stuff not many people ever would. And this…this was the only way I could cope.

"You don't need to say anything." Cade maneuvered me away from him a little. His face was level with mine as he swiped away the trailing tears. "All I asked was that you came to me, and you did." He moved his face closer, the green flecks in his blue eyes shining bright. "That was all I asked of you."

"You don't want to shout at me?" I asked, feeling so much like the insecure girl I knew I was deep down.

"No, baby." His lips curved into a grin. "I don't want to shout at you." He flicked his gaze down to my lips and then whispered his against mine in a gentle caress. My breath caught in my throat, and I pressed down harder. It had been too long since his last touch.

My cell rang out from my bag, but I ignored it as I pushed my hand through his hair and held him in place. I needed this. I needed him. More than he would ever know.

His gruff laugh cut us off. "You might wanna get that."

I groaned and reached over for my bag, seeing my mom's name on the screen of my cell. "Crap." I climbed off his lap and swung open the door, realizing where we were. "It's my mom."

Cade raised a brow at me, and slowly maneuvered himself out of his car, exuding a calm I could only dream of feeling. How the hell did he do that? "Come on," Cade said with a grin on his face. "I'll walk you inside."

He held his hand out to me, but I didn't take it. This wasn't the time or place, and when I shook my head at it, he looked down and frowned. "I keep forgetting." He blew out a breath, and we both started to walk across the lot. "I hate that I can't do the things with you that I really want to do."

I stared up at him. "And what would that be?"

He blinked down at me. "Dates…Movies, dinner, long walks on the beach."

"We don't live by a beach." I pursed my lips to hold in my laugh.

"You know what I mean." Cade pulled open the door to the diner. "All that romantic shit."

"Ahhh." I placed my hand on my chest. "Be still my beating heart."

Cade laughed, and I smiled wide at him. Only he could pull that smile out of me.

"Finally!" Mom shouted, and both of us whipped our heads around to face her as she practically ran across the diner to us. "We've been waiting forever. What took so long?"

I swallowed and opened my mouth, preparing to lie to her for the thousandth time, but Cade beat me to it. "My fault. I had some paperwork to finish off."

"Oh." Mom waved her hand in the air. "Never mind, you're here now." She twirled around and headed toward the right side of the diner where the booths were. "You joining us today, Cade?"

"Erm...I actually need to—"

"Good. Come sit."

I snickered at the way Mom cut him off. "You won't win with her. You should already know that."

Cade raised a brow and dipped down to whisper, "Why does this feel like I'm meeting your parents for the first time?" I rolled my eyes but couldn't hold in my snort. "Should I have brought flowers?"

"Shut up." I walked ahead of him and slid into the booth, but I wasn't expecting Cade to sit next to me.

"I'll go get you kids some drinks," Mom said, and spun back toward the main counter.

"Kids," Cade mumbled. "I haven't been a kid for nearly a decade."

I raised a brow and turned to face him. "You'll always be a kid to her."

"Yeah." His lips slowly spread into a smile. "I

spent so much time here growing up." He glanced around the diner and then stopped on my face. "Lola tutored me here when I was failing my classes. We'd always have a shake and fries after."

"Lola tutored you?" I asked, surprised by this tidbit of information.

Cade laughed and swiped his hand through his hair, making it stick up. "Yeah. I was failing English and math, and Lola was already working here and looking to tutor, so my mom hired her." He shook his head. "I never thought she'd end up with my dad."

"That's not how they met, though, is it?"

"Nah." Cade looked away from me as Mom walked across the diner. "They met when he was undercover."

I'd heard the stories of how they met, and couldn't help but wonder how Cade felt about it all. He was only a teenager at the time when his whole life was turned upside down.

"So…" Mom trailed off as she placed our drinks in front of us and slid in the booth opposite us. "How was your day?"

"Fine," I told her, the same thing I always said. There was never much to tell her about my day, mainly because I didn't want her to know. If I gave her a rundown of every little thing that happened at school, she'd never stop asking.

Mom nodded like she'd expected me to say that.

"Cade?"

"Same." I jumped when his hand landed on my knee, his fingers trailing up to my thigh and landing over my scars. I wondered if he knew where he was touching. "Aria got her personal best time on the track today."

"You did?" Mom asked, jumping in her seat and clapping her hands. "That's freaking awesome."

"What's awesome?" Sal's gruff voice asked. "Why's Cade here?"

"He dropped Aria off. I told him he had to stay."

"Gotcha," Sal said and slid into the booth next to Mom. "So what's awesome?"

"Aria got her personal best on the track," Mom told him, her eyes beaming, and for the first time, I didn't feel like I was a disappointment.

"Proud of you, Ri," Sal said. "You'll be off to the Olympics soon."

I ducked my head as my cheeks burned. It wasn't that they'd never said it before, I just…had never believed them. But one squeeze of Cade's hand on my leg told me he felt the same. Maybe this was when everything would change. Maybe being me would be enough and I wouldn't need the relief anymore.

Maybe…maybe I could start over and forget about the past.

If only it were easy.

Chapter Eleven

ARIA

"Ahoy, matey!" Asher shouted from where he was standing on the sofa. He held up his foam sword and readjusted his eye patch. "You walk the plank!"

"You walk the plank!" Belle shouted back, her own eye patch in place, but she also had a stuffed parrot attached to her shoulder using one of Lola's scarfs. They always battled for who was the captain of the Easton Ship, and almost always, Belle won the fight, and she made Asher walk the plank.

But today Asher was having none of it.

"I need to count the treasure, Belle!" He huffed and rolled his eyes.

"That's Captain Belle to you." She moved her head from side to side and planted her hands on her hips.

"Nu-uh, I'm the captain!" Asher shouted back and lunged across the sofa to where she was standing.

"Guys." I leaped forward, knowing a full-out war would ensue if I didn't step in. "You can both be captain."

"There's only one captain of this ship!" Belle raised her hands in the air. "And that's—"

"Me," a new voice said.

We all froze, our eyes widening, and then both kids launched themselves off the sofa and made a mad dash for the newcomer.

"Cade!" Belle shouted, her parrot wobbling precariously and nearly falling off her shoulder. "Tell Asher that, as the oldest Easton daughter, I get to be captain."

Cade reached down for Asher and threw him up onto his shoulders. "No can do, PB. I'm the captain."

"What?" She stomped her foot and twirled around to face me. "Aria, the boys are being mean to me!"

I raised my brows and tried my absolute hardest to keep a straight face. "Boys—"

"Why are boys so mean?" Belle asked, her little face starting to collapse, and I couldn't take it. Her bottom lip wobbled, and I practically ran toward her.

"Don't cry, Belle." I wrapped my arms around

her shoulders and brought her to my chest as I looked up at Cade and gave him my best death stare. "Apologize, Cade."

"What?" He pulled Asher off his shoulders and placed him on his hip. "What the hel—heck?"

"You made PB cry," Asher told him. "Youse mean."

"What? Me?" Cade pointed at his chest and blew out a big breath. "I'm sorry, PB. You can be the captain, okay?"

Belle sniffled and burrowed into my chest. "I'm not your friend." She hiccupped, and Cade's face dropped. If there was one thing that could make him give in, it was a girl crying, especially if said girl was his only sister.

"Ahhh, shit." He crouched down in front of us with Asher still attached to him. "I'm really sorry, PB. Please stop crying." Cade wrapped his free arm around Belle and me, and Asher wrapped his small arm around my head.

"Only if you take me somewhere," Belle said and slowly lifted her head. Her small hands wiped at the tears streaming down her face.

"Anywhere," Cade said, his large hand cupping the back of her head.

"I want to go to the fair."

"Okay," Cade told her, and as soon as the word came out of his mouth, she broke away from us, the tears having vanished. "I'll go get changed! Come on, Asher!" They both ran out of the room and up the stairs, screaming about all the cotton candy they were going to eat.

"I think…" Cade didn't move from his crouched position as he looked over at me. "I think I just got played."

I laughed as I stood, not able to resist moving closer to him and pushing my hand through his soft hair. "You did."

"Damn." He dipped his head back and placed his hands on my hips. "Well, guess I'm going to the fair." His lips quirked on one side. "Want to be my date?"

"Date?" I shook my head, but couldn't stop my own lips lifting. We hadn't been on a date, not unless it consisted of being inside his house or out on the track at school.

"Yeah, and we have the perfect cover." He slowly stood, towering over me with his six-foot-five height. "I promise I'll win you a stuffed animal."

I tapped my finger on my chin. "I want a corn dog too."

"You've got yourself a deal." He planted a kiss on the tip of my nose as footsteps pounded on the stairs and then Asher and Belle appeared, minus their pirate costumes.

"Ready," Belle declared, ushering Asher toward the door.

Cade strode across the living room. "Come on,"

he said, pulling the front door open. "Let's get you in the car."

Belle smiled up at him then ran out the door while Asher stayed close to Cade. I followed them out and locked the door behind me, and by the time I made it to the car on the driveway, Cade had strapped them both in.

I went to open the passenger door, but Cade beat me to it. His hand covered mine, and his front pressed against my back. My breath hitched at his closeness, and I shivered when his breath fanned across my neck. He always managed to make me forget who I was.

"Let me get that for you."

I closed my eyes at his deep voice and leaned against him. We couldn't do anything here, not with the kids watching, but I was going to soak in every one of his looks and touches while he was with us.

He pulled open the door and grasped my hip with his other hand, squeezed once, and then let me go. My cheeks burned as he walked around the car, and by the time I was slipping into the passenger seat, he was turning the engine on.

It didn't take us long to get to the fair, but it took nearly thirty minutes to find a parking spot. Everyone was here for the last weekend, and Friday evening made it even busier. Part of me worried we'd be seen, but hopefully, with the kids as a buffer, no one would question it if we were.

"Before we get out of the car," I said and twirled around in my seat to look at the kids. My lips flattened into a straight line, and I narrowed my eyes, making sure they knew how serious I was. "Belle, you stay with me at all times. Asher, you stay with Cade. You don't wander off. You don't get lost in the crowd. You don't—"

"Aria," Cade interrupted, and I flicked my gaze to his. "They'll stay with us."

"I'm just making sure they know the rules." I rolled my eyes and pushed out of the car, making out like it wasn't a big deal, but it was. The last time I'd come to a fair I'd been seven years old. The bright lights and rides had lured me in, but not as much as they had to my dad. He'd been fascinated by them and forgotten all about his daughter. He'd left me alone for hours, only finding me when the fair was almost closed. The day was burned into my brain like so many others that involved my dad.

I took Belle's hand, and we walked side by side with Cade who had Asher on his shoulders. Belle was talking a mile a minute, but the closer we got to the entrance, the less I could hear what she was saying over the buzzing ringing in my ears.

My breathing picked up, almost coming in pants when Cade bought us tickets, and then we were standing in the middle of the fair, the scent of cotton candy and corn dogs surrounding us. The rhythm of laughter mixed in with the loudness of voices and sounds of the rides, but it was the bright lights flashing that had me closing my eyes and wishing I was anywhere else but here.

"Ow, Aria, you're hurting my hand."

I flung my eyes open and blinked down at Belle. "Sorry," I managed to croak out. Her other hand was encased in Cade's, so I let go and backed away a step. Maybe this wasn't such a good idea after all.

Cade's gaze was burning a path on the side of my face, but I couldn't look up at him. I was afraid of what he'd see. Afraid he'd realize how damaged I was. Afraid he'd find out I was unfixable.

"What ride do you want to go on first?" Cade asked, and they both shouted something different. He spun around and pushed through the crowd, and I followed after them, my stomach sinking at the thought of losing them here.

Everything was too much for me, but I tried my hardest to smile and encourage a different feeling than the one I currently had. I watched Cade put them both on one of the kiddie rides, and stood off to the side, not taking my eyes off them.

"Aria," Cade said as he halted next to me. There were other kids getting on the ride, but I kept my attention on Belle and Asher who sat up front. "Baby, look at me."

"I can't," I croaked out. "I hate this."

His hand grasped mine and pulled it toward him, hiding it between his waist and the fence. No one would be able to see we were holding hands if they saw us.

"What happened?" I could hear the hitch in his voice. I could sense the concern.

"I was seven the last time I came to the fair." I kept my gaze locked on Belle and Asher as the ride started. "Dad brought me. He promised me we'd have fun." I stuttered a breath. "But then he…he… he forgot I was with him." My free hand clutched against my chest and rested above my racing heart. "He left me alone for five hours on a fairground just like this one." A tear streamed down my face, and I finally plucked up the nerve to look over at Cade. "I know he was sick, but I…"

"Doesn't mean you don't resent him for it," Cade finished for me, and I nodded.

I didn't need anyone to tell me it was going to be okay. I didn't need Cade to fill me with promises of what would happen from now on, and he never did that. He didn't make out like everything was unicorns and rainbows. He was just there…always there.

"I think you need to create new fair memories," Cade declared as the ride came to a stop. He brought my hand up to his mouth, placed a kiss on my knuckles, and then let go. "First stop is corn dogs and winning prizes." He waited until I nodded then stepped forward to help get the kids off the ride.

The small smile on my face started to get bigger, and by the time Cade turned back around and grinned over at me, it was a real smile. I kept to myself in fear of being judged, but Cade never judged the way I was feeling, and he never talked it to death. He simply found a solution and got right on with it.

"I'm hungry," Belle said as her hand slipped into mine.

I groaned and put my hand to my stomach. "Me too." I flicked my gaze behind us. Cade was putting Asher back on his shoulders, and I decided right then and there I was going to throw caution to the wind. I was going to enjoy the next few hours and forget about my past. "Race you! Loser buys the corn dogs!"

Belle squealed as I pulled her with me, but in only a couple of paces, she realized what I was doing and helped weave us through the crowd. I turned my head as my feet pounded the ground, spotting Cade only a few paces behind us. He winked, causing butterflies to take flight in my stomach.

And I knew there and then.

I knew, in that very moment, I was in love with Cade Easton.

———

ARIA

"I feel like I don't see you anymore," Hope whined as I stood from our position under the bleachers. "We never get girl time."

I collected my trash and raised a brow at her. "That's because you're always taking off with your sister. You've had more days off school than you've been here."

Hope puffed out a breath and let her head drop back. "I know. I'm so behind in my classes, and I swear, I'm failing like half of them."

I bit my bottom lip as I stared over at the wall of windows I knew was Cade's office. I couldn't see inside because he had the blinds closed, but I knew he was in there. I hadn't spoken to him properly since he dropped us off after we went to the fair a few days ago. We'd texted a couple of times, but it wasn't the same as hearing his voice.

There were only thirty minutes left of lunch, and I wanted to spend as much time as I could with Cade. We had track practice later today, but Mom was picking me up right after because she wasn't working, which meant I wouldn't see Cade again until this weekend at Brody and Lola's cookout.

"You need to talk to Lisha. She can't keep taking you out of school like this."

"I know." Hope stood, her lips pulled down. "I need to go see the counselor too. If you're going to talk to Mr. Easton, I may as well head in and see her now."

I nodded, afraid she'd ask why I was going to see Cade. I could cover easily and say it was because of track, but Hope could sniff out a lie like she was a cadaver dog. She had a sixth sense for these things.

We both walked into the school, and I gripped her arm. "I'm serious, Hope. You need to talk to her. Otherwise, you're not going to graduate."

Hope's eyes flashed at me, the bags under them letting me know something else was going on. I'd been so inside my head lately that I'd forgotten all about her. She was my best friend, but I wasn't treating her like it.

"Next week," I told her. "Next week, me and you, movie night at my place."

"Yeah?" Her lips pulled up into a smile.

"Yeah."

"Awesome!" She high-fived me, and I blinked. We never high-fived. "I'm gonna go sort my life out. Catch you later?"

"You betcha." I watched as she walked down the hall, waited a second, and then spun around. Cade's office wasn't far from this part of the school, so I made it there within a couple of minutes, which would give us twenty minutes until the bell rang for class.

I stopped outside his office. The door was closed, and I wondered if he'd left in the time it took me to get here. What if he was busy and didn't want to see me? What if—I shook my head. There was no point in me wondering about the what-ifs. I needed to stop overthinking and knock on the door.

Pulling in a deep breath to try and calm myself, I knocked. "Come in!" his gruff voice shouted, so I slowly opened up the door. Cade was staring down at something on his desk, a frown on his face. I stayed silent, waiting for him to look up at me as I stepped inside and closed the door behind me.

All of his blinds were closed, so not an ounce of sunlight streamed in the room. The only window not covered was the one on his door, so I slowly turned around and pulled the blind down, then leaned my back against it.

Cade still wasn't looking my way, but the longer I stared at him, the shallower my breaths became. He had on his shirt and pants, the top button of the shirt undone and the sleeves rolled up to his elbows, showcasing his tattoos.

He finally glanced up, his gaze landing right on mine. "Aria." The way his tongue rolled over the letters in my name had my eyes closing, and when I opened them back up, he was leaning back in his chair.

My hand fumbled behind me to find the lock, and the click of it rang out in the room. His nostrils flared at the sound—his body knew what was going to happen. I pushed off the door, let my bag drop to the floor, and sauntered over to him. He watched each one of my steps with rapt attention, and when I was in touching distance, he reached out for me. I went willingly, not able to deny him. I wasn't sure I would ever be able to deny him.

"I fuckin' missed touchin' you, baby."

I groaned as his hands gripped my waist, his fingers curling underneath the edge of my T-shirt. "Me too," I murmured, and pushed my hand through his hair. His head was level with my chest, but he kept his gaze fixated on my eyes. He didn't look away once as his hands pushed higher, taking my T-shirt with them.

We'd kissed and got a little hot and heavy, but we'd never gone any further than that. Today, though…today I wanted to beg him to touch me in places no one ever had.

"We shouldn't be doing this," he told me, dragging my T-shirt over my chest. I lifted my arms for him to pull it over my head. I lost sight of his eyes for a second, but as soon as he threw my T-shirt on the floor, I looked back at him.

"I know," I told him, resisting the urge to cover my chest. The black lace bra was covering half of my breasts, but I knew he could see my nipples through the thin material.

"Tell me to stop," Cade pleaded, his thumbs reaching for my nipples. I groaned as they made contact. "Tell me, Aria. Tell me to stop."

"I can't," I whispered, pushing closer to him.

"Fuck." He stood so quickly it made my head spin. "Why can't I resist you?" He didn't want an answer, and even if he did, I couldn't give him one. I had no idea why my heart beat faster around him. I had no idea why the thought of him never touching me again made me feel like I would break apart into a thousand tiny pieces.

Cade reached around me, and I widened my eyes as he shoved all the papers off his desk and then placed me on it. He pushed between my legs, his lips connecting with my exposed shoulder. I let my head drop to the side as he trailed a path up my neck. He waited a heartbeat, and then slammed his lips against mine.

My stomach dipped and my legs wrapped around his waist, unable to resist touching him. I groaned when his hand reached behind me and undid my bra, then grasped his hair tighter as he pulled his lips off mine and moved to my nipples. He pulled one into his mouth, flicking his tongue over it as he ran his thumb over the other one.

All too quickly he was pulling back, leaving my chest heaving. He didn't take his eyes off me as he backed away a step, taking his fill. "I need to touch you." It was part statement, part plea, and there was no way I would deny him.

The bell rang out for the next class, but neither of us moved to exit. Instead, Cade undid the next button on his shirt. My stomach dipped at each one being undone, and when it was finally completely open, he yanked it off and threw it on the floor next to my T-shirt.

"I don't have a class," he told me, stepping back between my legs and reaching for my jeans. "But even if I did, there's no way I'd walk away from you right now." His one hand trailed up my stomach and between my breasts, stopping on the side of my neck. "No way in hell."

I gulped as he fingers pulled down the zipper of my jeans, and choked on a breath as his hand pushed beneath my panties.

"Cade," I moaned. "I've never been touched—"

"I know, baby." He pushed against me, making my back hit his desk. "And that just turns me on even fuckin' more."

My back bowed as he ran his finger through my slit, hitting the bundle of nerves I was sure would make me explode within a second. His lips trailed over my breast and moved back to my nipple, lapping at it.

"Fuck, Cade, I can't…"

"Mmmm, say that again, baby."

"What?" I asked, looking down at him. I didn't think he could get any hotter than he already was, but seeing his lips against my skin and his tattoo-covered chest was my undoing.

"Fuck. Say fuck again. You sound so goddamn hot when you curse."

A blush burned at my cheeks, and I opened my mouth, about to tell him I wouldn't say it again, but he pushed a finger inside me, drawing a "Fuck," from me.

"Yes." He pushed his finger in and out, and I winced at the pinch. "You're so goddamn tight."

"Cade…" I wrapped my arms around his waist, searching for his lips with mine. "It's too much. I can't…you can't…"

"Close your eyes, baby," he whispered, pressing his chest against mine and laying me flat on his desk again. "Feel it. Feel my finger inside you." He kissed my lips gently. "Feel my lips against yours." I pulled in a breath. "Feel my fingers against your nipple."

I closed my eyes and did just as he said. I let myself feel it. I let myself bask in his thumb rubbing against my clit as he pumped his finger in and out of me, widening me with his thrusts. I let myself feel his lips against my skin, and his fingers pinching my nipple.

I let it all in, but I wasn't sure I'd survive it.

Something started low in my stomach, a fizzle of some kind, and then without warning, I exploded. I screamed his name, but his mouth cut me off, and I forgot about everything with him against me. I forgot about who we were. I forgot about where we were.

"Cade," I gasped as he slowed his thumb on my clit, my orgasm drifting away. "I can't even..." I didn't know what to say. He'd blown my mind, and I was speechless.

"Say you'll stay with me on Saturday night." His finger didn't move from inside me as my walls pulsated around it. His forehead leaned against mine as he said, "Say you'll stay the night and let me love you the way you deserve to be loved."

I heard what he was saying, and there wasn't a doubt in my mind as I nodded and told him, "Yes."

Chapter Twelve

CADE

If there was one thing my dad and Lola knew how to do, it was a cookout. I hadn't been to one where everyone attended for what felt like years, and when I really thought about it, I realized the last time had been when I was a college senior. Back then, Aria hadn't been in attendance.

Aria.

My cheeks hurt with how wide I grinned. My mind immediately took me back to the image of her being spread out on my desk, half-naked, my lips whispering over her skin, and my fingers between her legs. Fuck. I was getting hard just thinking about it.

She'd promised to stay over at my house tonight, but part of me wondered if it was a good idea. She was seventeen, and my student, but damn if I could resist the temptation when it came to her. She had me tied up in knots I couldn't undo, no matter how much I tried. I was crossing boundaries I had no right to cross, but I couldn't stop.

She was my kryptonite, and I had no cure.

I picked at the label on the beer bottle, my gaze swinging around the backyard. Asher and Belle were running around chasing each other, Dad was manning the grill with Sal next to him, and Lola, Jan, and Aria were in the kitchen. I couldn't see her from where I was, which made getting up from the table and walking away from Dad's team—Jord, Kyle, Ryan, and Ford—all the easier.

The guys didn't look my way as I crossed the yard and walked past Dad and Sal. They were talking about some case they were all working, which meant I didn't have a place in their conversation. I was used to hearing them talk about cases since I moved in with Dad when I was fifteen. They'd trained and worked together. They were a family, anyone from the outside looking in could see that.

But they weren't *my* family. Not really. They'd been there for me when I needed them, but only one person in this house knew what had happened while I was away. I was keeping a secret from them all, much like Aria was. She'd shared hers with me —through no choice of her own—but I hadn't told her mine. Maybe tonight would be the night I confessed what happened. Maybe I could confide in her and strip myself bare the way she had with me.

I heard her laughter before I stepped into the kitchen, but I hadn't been expecting her to be walking into the living room. Jan and Lola were preparing some side dishes, paying no mind to me as I moved through the kitchen.

I caught sight of Aria as she headed for the stairs, and I drifted toward her. If she knew I was following her, she didn't give any indication as she went up the stairs. Her ass swayed with each of her movements, and I groaned at the sight.

My stomach dipped as I got to the top of the stairs, and she finally looked back at me. "Are you following me, Cade?" She raised her brow and propped her hand on her hip. I'd never seen her in a dress before, not since she was a little girl, but fuck, she looked hot.

"Maybe I am." I stalked toward her, the beer bottle hanging from my fingers. "What would you say to that?"

She bit down on her plump bottom lip as her gaze tracked over me. My light-denim ripped jeans hung low on my hips, and my black T-shirt showed both tattooed arms.

"I'd say…" Her chest expanded on a breath as I closed more of the distance between us. There were only a few steps separating us now, and she backed herself against the wall between the bathroom and my bedroom.

"What would you say?" I asked, taking another step. I leaned my arm on the wall above her head, not an inch of my body touching hers. Her lips parted, and her tongue swiped along them, calling to me, begging me to touch them.

"I'd say…" She reached her hand out and flattened her palm against my stomach, her fingers trailing over the contour of my abs. "You can always follow me."

"Yeah?" I couldn't stop my hand from grasping her waist, and my fingers connected with the skin showing there. I had no idea what kind of dress this was, but it was calling to me on all sorts of levels. "What would you say if I touched you?"

"Touched me where?" she whispered, her eyes flaring. She was thinking about the other day too. I could tell from the way she shuffled on the spot, and I'd bet my bottom dollar her panties were soaked.

I whispered my fingers across her hips and bent down a little to lift her dress. The dark material bunched in my hand, and then I was between her legs, a grin spreading across my face because I'd been right.

From this position, I could feel the scars on her thighs, and I hesitated. In my office, I hadn't pulled her jeans down far enough to touch or see them, and part of me had forgotten.

"Cade," her soft voice pleaded, and she locked her thighs around my hand, stopping my momentum but keeping me there. "I'm sorry."

"No." I shook my head and pushed my body flush with hers. "You don't need to say that, not to me." My eyes stayed focused on hers, not willing to look away. "You never have to apologize for the scars you hold, whether I can see them or not." I pulled in a breath and clutched her thigh. "They're a part of you, and I don't want to change that."

"But—"

"Aria?" I yanked myself away from her at the sound of Jan's voice. Her footsteps followed a second later. "Are you coming to help, or what?"

"I…" Aria shook her head and cleared her throat, backing away from me and toward the stairs. "I'm coming, Mom."

I quirked my lips and winked as I whispered, "Not yet, baby."

"Cade!" she whisper-shouted, her eyes widening. "Stop it."

"Who are you talking to?" Jan asked, and then her face appeared. "Oh, hey, Cade. What are you doing up here?"

I pointed my beer toward the bathroom. "Waiting for Aria to finish up."

Jan's gaze batted between the two of us, and she frowned. That frown said so much more than I was willing to admit, but Jan quickly schooled her features. "Come on, food is ready."

I didn't look at Aria again as I walked into the bathroom and waited for a couple of minutes for them to be back downstairs. That had been close, but I couldn't bring myself to feel bad for it. I couldn't bring myself to care one bit, because all that mattered right now was Aria and me. All I cared about was when I would be able to touch her next, and when I would be able to hear her soft voice again.

By the time I made it into the backyard, everyone was sitting around the table. Asher and Belle were either side of Aria. Ford took the open seat next to Belle with Jord next to him. Jan was next to Asher and Sal with Dad next to them, which left one open seat between Lola and Kyle. I was on the opposite end to Aria, but maybe that was a good thing. Maybe if we were kept apart for a little while, I wouldn't be so obvious.

Conversation flowed between everyone as we passed around bowls of sides and meat Dad had grilled, but it wasn't until I heard Belle say, "Do you have a girlfriend, Cade?" that I nearly choked on the potato salad in my mouth.

"Wh-what?" I couldn't help but flick my gaze to Aria before looking at Belle, but Aria was too busy staring down at her plate.

"Do you have a girlfriend?" Belle repeated and rolled her eyes at me.

"I…erm…"

"Oh snap!" Jord shouted. "Little sister has just outed you." I blinked at him and his small Afro that was faded from his neck up.

"Outed me?" My pulse quickened, and I kept my gaze on anything but Aria. I'd missed half of the conversation, so I wasn't even sure what was going on.

"You got a secret girlfriend we don't know about, son?" Dad asked, and I turned to look at him. His brows were raised, waiting for my answer, but I wasn't sure what I should say. All eyes were on me, but I'd never squirmed the way I did right then.

"I…I've met someone."

"You have?" Lola asked, her hand gripping on to my arm in excitement. "Tell us all about her."

"She…" I swallowed and pushed some food around my plate with my fork. "She's different."

"Different how?" Lola asked.

"I…" I blew out a breath and pushed my hand through my hair, pulling on it to try and distract myself, but it was no use. My gaze moved to Aria, and her eyes were focused on me. The light-brown orbs were pulling me in, and nothing I did could make me look away. "I've never felt like this before. It's different with her. Just…more."

"More?" Lola asked, but her voice was far away. I was in a land of my own where only Aria and I existed. A world where no one cared she was seventeen, and I was twenty-five. A world where it didn't matter that she was my student. A world where love trumped everything, and rules and regulations didn't matter.

"Yeah…more," I repeated to Lola, and finally looked away from Aria.

Lola's smile was so big I was sure it was going to break her face. "Are you in love with her, Cade?"

I didn't answer her. I wasn't sure what I felt, but there was no way I was going to admit anything to Lola when the woman I couldn't stop thinking about was sitting at the other end of the table.

"Leave the boy alone, Lola-Girl," Sal grunted. "He don't wanna talk about his fluffy feelings 'round a table full of men."

"Yeah, Mama," Asher said, his small voice trying to sound deeper than it was. "We men."

Lola laughed. "I know you are, honey." Asher puffed his chest out at her words. She leaned toward me and whispered, "I hope I get to meet this girl soon."

I nodded and stared back at Aria, finding her gaze right away. It was on the tip of my tongue to blurt out she'd already met her, but…I couldn't. We were keeping secrets from everyone, and all it reminded me about was the secret I was keeping from Aria.

———

ARIA

The cookout was different from all the others I'd attended. Usually, I helped Lola and Mom make the food. I'd set the table with Belle and then play with Asher, but today was different. Today Cade was here, and every little look was making me more and more on edge about what would come when the sun set and the darkness took over.

Mom and Sal had left an hour ago to close up the diner. Lola had put Asher and Belle to bed, leaving me in the backyard with Uncle Brody and all his friends.

I'd spoken to all of them, but it was always Ford who I had real conversations with. I wasn't sure if it was because he was younger than the rest by more than a decade. He'd just turned thirty, which meant he was closer in age to Cade and me than his teammates.

"So, senior year, huh?" Ford asked, not looking at me but at Cade as he helped Uncle Brody clean the grill. "You decided if you're going to college yet?"

I glanced over his face. His nose was straight apart from a small crook in it. I shrugged. "Probably. Mom said I should try and get a track scholarship but…I don't know."

"You run track?" Ford swiveled in his seat, giving me his full attention. His hazel eyes focused on me.

"Yeah." I tilted my head to the side. "I thought I told you that last time I saw you?"

Ford shook his head. "I would have remembered that." He shuffled forward on his seat, balancing on the edge. "Cade your coach?"

"I…" I could feel the burning of my cheeks at the mention of his name and what we'd done the last day I'd had practice. The memory of how he'd made me feel was etched into my mind, and I squirmed at the thought of it. "Yeah." My voice was small, almost a breath, and from the way Ford's brows rose, he definitely noticed.

His gaze tracked over me. He drank in my face and then moved down to the hands I had clutched in my lap. I felt like I was being interrogated silently. He was taking in every bit of my body language, and I had no idea what conclusion he was coming to.

"Aria?" Cade's voice broke through our stare-off. "You need a ride home?"

I blinked. "Yes, please."

Ford stood, the top of his head only a couple of inches shorter than Cade's. "I'm heading that way, I can give her a ride."

Cade tilted his head and looked between the two of us, but there was nothing I could say. I wasn't good in situations like these, especially not surrounded by five alpha-male DEA agents. I was out of my depth, so I stayed silent.

"I got it. I take her home after practice anyway, so I know the way," Cade told Ford and positioned his body so he was partly in front of me. The move was an obvious one, and I felt like I needed to tell him to stop, but that would make it all the more obvious.

"You do?" Ford asked, but his voice wasn't light and airy like it had been all night. It was calculating, and he wasn't only assessing my reaction to Cade now, but Cade's reaction to me.

"Yeah, I—"

"Aria? What are you still doing here?" Lola asked, and my breath whooshed out of me. The tension was building, but with Lola as a buffer, it would be sure to dissipate—I hoped. "I thought Cade was taking you home?" Lola stood at the edge of the semicircle we'd made, glancing between Cade and Ford.

"I'm gonna take her home," Ford told her.

Lola snorted. "I don't think so. You've drunk way too many beers."

"Yeah!" Kyle shouted, inserting himself into the conversation. "You can't break the law when you *are* the law, bro." He ran his hand through his hair and winked at me.

"What he said," Lola told him, pointing at Kyle.

"Cade can take her." Lola moved between Cade and me and flung her arm over my shoulders. "You're good with that, right, sweetheart?"

I tried to keep my face straight, but it was a hard task to do because I was more than okay with Cade taking me home—to *his* home. "Yeah."

"Okay." She pulled me away from Cade and Ford. "Go say g'night to Uncle Brody. I'll get Cade to meet you out front."

I did as she said and walked over to Uncle Brody, who was watching the scene with interest, but as soon as I moved up the steps, he opened his arms to me. "You heading out, baby girl?" his gruff voice asked.

"Yeah." I laid my head on his chest and pulled in a deep breath. I'd never doubted whether I could trust Brody. From the first time I met him, I could sense he'd keep me safe. I'd only ever felt like that with a handful of people in my life, and they were all standing in this backyard.

There'd been a time I was sure Mom would keep me safe, but she'd ignored so many signs, so many red flags she should have battled through. I didn't doubt Mom loved and cared for me, she just…didn't pay attention.

Uncle Brody planted a kiss on the top of my head and pulled back. "Love ya, baby girl."

"Love you too, Uncle Brody." I took one last look on the lawn where Ford and Lola were arguing over something, but Cade was watching me. His dark-blue eyes pierced mine in the dim light, and as soon as I backed away a step, he took one closer to me.

He stalked toward me like a lion who had his prey in sight, and as soon as I was back in the house, I spun around and headed for the front door. He caught up with me and his hands grasped my waist as I pulled it open. "Let's get out of here."

I couldn't agree more, so I nodded and let him lead me toward his car where he opened up the passenger door for me. He shut the door behind me and rushed around to his side, started the engine, and pulled out of the drive. He halted when he was on the road and looked back at the house. I frowned, seeing Ford in the front doorway staring at us.

"What's going on?" I asked. Ford had insisted he take me home, and now he was watching us with his head tilted to the side like he was trying to figure out a puzzle.

Cade didn't answer me. Instead, he revved the engine, and Ford stepped forward. His brows were pulled down, the expression on his face moving from inquisitive to furious. I flicked my gaze between Cade and Ford, wondering what the hell was going on. I opened my mouth, about to repeat my earlier question, but Cade sped off.

I clutched on to my belt and held my breath at

how fast he took the corner. "Cade, slow down." He ignored me, mumbling something under his breath, so I clasped on to his arm. "Please, slow down."

"Fuck!" He slowed right down and shook his head, his hands gripping the steering wheel so tight his knuckles were turning white. His chest heaved on a breath, and I stared at a bead of sweat as it trailed down his temple. He was on edge, more on edge than I'd ever seen him. Was this because of what we planned to do tonight? Or was it the way Ford had acted?

"Cade?" I whispered, trying to gain his attention.

He didn't say anything to me as he took the turn for his street, only now he was much slower than he had been moments ago.

"I'm sorry, baby," he croaked out.

"Sorry?" I squeezed my hand on his arm, trying to understand what was going on, but I was more confused than ever. "What's going on?"

"I…" Cade blinked several times and pulled into his own driveway. He turned the engine off, but he didn't make to move out of his car. "There's something I need to tell you." He kept his gaze focused on the windshield. "I…fuck, I don't even know where to start."

I leaned back in my seat and unclipped the belt, giving him time to get himself together. My stomach churned with what he was about to say, nerves flowing through me at the speed of light. His features were screwed up, his gaze flicking all over the place. "Start at the beginning," I told him.

I wasn't sure what I thought he was going to say, but it definitely wasn't, "It was my senior year at college." I swallowed at the roughness of his voice but didn't take my gaze off him. "We were all heading to a party on the other side of town." He paused and scrubbed his hand through his hair. "My girlfriend at the time was in the passenger seat, my two best friends and roommates in the back." Cade shook his head, and I couldn't bear the agony etched onto his features.

"Cade—"

"I forgot my wallet, so I went back inside for it." He slammed his palm on the steering wheel. "If I wouldn't have forgotten it, they'd still be here." *Still be here?* "I still don't understand...I just...I remember the light being green and driving over the intersection and then..." Cade winced and rubbed his shoulder. "Something hit us. The metal crunched as we flipped, tires squealed, and then the smell of gas when we finally stopped."

"Cade," I whispered, and it took everything in me not to climb over to him.

"It's my fault. If we were ten seconds earlier or ten seconds later—"

"You can't think like that, you—"

Cade's abrupt laugh cut me off, and he turned

his head to face me. "I *can* think like that because I was fuckin' driving. I woke up with a cut on my head, a dislocated shoulder, and three dead bodies surrounding me."

I leaned up on my knees and placed my hands on either side of his face. "That doesn't make it your fault." I clenched my fingers, trying to push my point home. "You said something else hit you?"

"Yeah." His voice had lost all the hatred and was now tired. "A truck."

"Then it's not your fault."

"But if I'd have—"

"No." I brought my leg over the center console and pushed between Cade's chest and the steering wheel, not letting go of his face. "You can't control the actions of people around you. You can only control yours." I shook my head. "The what-ifs will kill you, Cade. The what-ifs will destroy your soul."

I knew better than anyone about the what-ifs. I'd mulled over them for nearly ten years, but not once had they made a bit of difference.

"Ford helped me," Cade said. "He was in town visiting his cousin and came to the hospital. He helped me...he...he was there when no one else was."

"You're close with Ford then?" Cade wrapped his arms around me and buried his head in my chest, mumbling something I couldn't understand. "Cade?"

He shook his head and held me tighter, finally moving his face. "I don't want to talk about Ford." His stare met mine. "I don't want to talk about what happened that night."

"Okay..."

"I just need you, Aria. I need you more than I've needed anything in my entire life."

I stuttered a breath and placed my hand on his face. "You have me, Cade. You've always had me."

———

CADE

"You have me, Cade. You've always had me."

Her words flowed through me, and there was nothing I could do but slam my lips onto hers. I forgot all about what we'd been talking about. I forgot about the scene in my head of the crash. I forgot about what Ford had done for me afterward. All I concentrated on was the feel of Aria's body pressed against me and the way her lips meshed with mine.

I pushed open the driver's side door and grabbed my keys from the ignition, all the while not letting go of her.

"You can put me down," she whispered as her hands gripped my shoulders tighter.

"No." I stopped at my front door and pushed

the key in the lock. "I don't intend to put you down unless it's on my bed." I was being forward, but there was nothing I could do to stop it. I needed her more than anything else at that moment, and I wasn't going to shy away from it.

Her small smile became bigger as I stepped inside and locked the door behind us. I didn't bother to turn any of the lights on. I headed up the stairs and toward my room.

Aria rocked her hips against me, and I stumbled. "Fuck, baby." She didn't let up, not even when I placed her on the bed. "You're a goddamn siren," I told her, sucking against her neck and then licking to soothe the pain.

"Cade," she groaned, and I pulled back to stare at her. Her dark-red hair was fanned out around her, and she looked like a fuckin' angel. Her chest heaved with each breath, and the dip in her dress pulled down just enough so I could see her cleavage.

I reached for the bottom of my T-shirt and pulled it over my head, loving the way her eyes drank me in. Her small hand reached for me as she sat up, and the pads of her fingers ran down the contours of my abs.

"You like that?" I asked her, backing away a little so I could stand.

She shuffled down the bed so she was right on the edge. "I do." She flattened her palm and whispered it up to my chest, standing as she did. Her hand stopped over my fast-beating heart as she looked up at me. "Show me, Cade." She pressed her lips to my chest, and my nostrils flared. "Show me how much you want me right now."

She didn't need to ask me twice. I wanted her more than anything I'd ever had, and I was going to show her just how much.

I drifted the pad of my finger across her collarbone, down between her breasts, and gripped the zipper that held her dress onto her body. My fingers shook as I started to pull it down, exposing more of her creamy skin. I'd never been nervous, but she was making my emotions go haywire.

My other hand pushed her hair aside, and once the zipper was completely undone, I pushed the straps off her shoulders and relished in the way the material fell off her body.

"Fuck. Me." I pulled in a breath as I stared down at her, enthralled with the way her waist dipped in and the curve of her hips. But it was her bare chest that had my full attention.

I dipped down and placed a kiss to each of her nipples, then licked from her breastbone, all the way to her belly button, and kneeled down in front of her. The edge of her light-pink panties called to me, and I closed my teeth over the edge.

"Cade." Her voice was nothing but a breathy moan, and when I looked up at her and placed my hands on either side of her hips, I knew I'd never be the same after this. She was burrowing her way into my heart, and there was nothing I could do to stop it.

I pulled her panties down with my teeth, exposing her fully to me. They dropped to the floor, and I pushed her back so she'd land on the bed.

She laughed as she bounced back up, her hands coming out to help her fall. My gaze landed on her thighs, and the scars marring her skin. They started just above her knees and went right up to the edge of her pussy. I hated them. I hated them because they showed her inner turmoil. But I loved them because they were part of her. I was at war with them, but I needed to put them aside and concentrate on her, and only her.

I flicked my gaze up to her, and she was watching me carefully. "You're so fuckin' beautiful, Aria." Her cheeks tinted red, and I grinned at the blush. I trailed my finger from her ankle, over her knee, and up to her pussy, dipping inside her folds and groaning at her wetness.

"God, Cade," she groaned, her hands gripping on to the comforter of my bed. "Don't stop."

I had no intention of stopping. None whatsoever. I leaned forward and placed each hand over her inner thighs. My palms felt the scars on them as I pushed my face between her legs and licked her pussy.

Her hand pushed through my hair and gripped

so tightly my scalp burned, but I grinned at it. It turned me the hell on when she did that, so I licked her again, this time pulling her clit into my mouth and sucking on it.

"Ahhhh." Her legs locked around my head, but I didn't let up. I lapped at her like she was the last thing I was ever going to eat, and didn't stop until her legs were shaking, and she was screaming, "It's too much!"

My hand drifted to her chest, and I tweaked one of her nipples then sucked her clit one last time, knowing it was exactly what she needed to fall off the edge of the cliff and let go.

Her back bowed off the bed, and I moved with her, let her clit go, and did one final lick to eek her orgasm out even more. Her hand slowly let go of my hair, her body crashing as she rode the high and aftereffects, but I wasn't done with her yet. I needed to show her exactly how I felt about her, and there was only one way to do that.

I stood, started to pull the zipper down on my jeans, and kept my gaze locked with her face. Her light-brown eyes opened, sleepy and satisfied, but as soon as they connected with mine, they sparked.

"No." She shook her head, and I stopped pulling my zipper down, frowning at her as she sat up and shuffled to the edge of the bed. "That's my job."

Her small hand covered mine over my zipper

then pushed it aside. She dipped her head back, staring up at me, the only sound in the room our heavy breathing and the metal of my zipper as she tugged it all the way down.

I lifted my hand and placed it on the side of her face, my thumb rubbing back and forth. My stomach dipped, and I couldn't believe I was standing here, watching her undress me. How the hell had that happened?

"Aria," I whispered. I didn't know what else to say. I wasn't sure there was anything I *could* say.

She grasped each side of my jeans over my hips and pulled, revealing my boxer briefs. Her fingers whispered over my erection covered by the black material, and I closed my eyes at the sensation.

"Cade? Look at me."

I did as she commanded, and heaved in a sharp breath at the way she stared up at me. There was nothing but confidence in the way her shoulders pulled back and the way her stare stayed on mine.

Slowly—*oh so goddamn slowly*—she pulled my boxer briefs down, and my erection sprang free. Her hand curled around the base, and I wasn't sure I could take much of her touch before I'd blow my load.

"Baby." I leaned forward and placed my hands on either side of her, but she didn't let go of my cock. Her grip was firm and demanding. "I need you so bad right now."

She groaned, her eyes closing. "Yessss."

My lips connected with her neck as I wrapped an arm around her waist and brought her back down to the bed. My body covered hers fully, but I fuckin' loved it. I loved how small she was. I loved how I could encompass her and keep her safe.

Her hands gripped my back, keeping me glued to her, and I readjusted my position so the head of my cock was at her entrance. There was no going back once we eradicated this line. We'd always have this, no matter what.

"I'm on the pill," she blurted out, and I widened my eyes. She'd gotten me so lost inside of her, I hadn't even thought about it.

I pressed my forehead to hers and pushed slowly, whispering, "It's okay," as she winced. "Relax, baby. It's just you and me." Her stare connected with mine. "It'll always be you and me," I promised her.

Her chest expanded, her nipples scraping over my pecs as she pulled in a breath. "Do it," she urged.

I thrust some more and tensed at how tight she was. I wanted to take my time. I wanted to relish every second of us in my bed, but I wasn't sure how long I could hold on for. The tip of my cock hit her barrier, and I paused for a second. Once this was gone, there really would be no turning back. But one look down at her had my mind made up, and I pushed my hips forward, breaking through it.

Aria gripped me tighter, her legs wrapping around my waist, and I hated the tears rolling down the side of her face and into her hair. "Baby, we can stop—"

"No." Her voice was a determined whisper. There was no doubting the word she'd spoken. "Keep going."

I swallowed and blew out a breath. "Okay, but if it's too much…"

Her lips pulled up into the sweetest smile, and if I had been standing, it would have knocked me off my feet. "Everything is always too much with you, Cade."

I grinned and pulled back slightly, then pushed back in. Her breath hitched, but I wasn't sure if it was the pain she was feeling or the pleasure from my thumb as I pressed it against her clit. The only way to keep her relaxed was to get her to orgasm again. The thought of her pussy pulsating around my cock spurred me on, and I thrust faster.

"Fuck," I spat, sitting up more and gripping her waist with my free hand as I stared down at her. She was so fuckin' hot spread out on my bed, letting me take part of her she'd never given anyone else.

Her eyes closed, her hands gripping my biceps, her nails puncturing my skin. "More."

She didn't have to tell me twice, so I thrust even faster, my thumb rubbing her clit so quick my arm started to cramp. Her eyes rolled back in her head, her hair a matted mess on her face, and then I felt it. Her pussy clamped around my cock, and I let go. I let go of what I'd been trying to keep at bay. I let myself feel every fuckin' inch of her as my balls tightened. My head dipped back, the muscles in my neck tensing, my teeth clenching together, and fuck...I'd never felt anything like it. It was heaven and hell all rolled into one. Fire and ice mixing and compounding.

It was everything, and it was all because of the girl beneath me.

Aria.

It would always be Aria.

Chapter Thirteen

CADE

My lips lifted into a smile before my eyes even cracked open. Aria was attached to my chest, her soft breathing echoing around us, and her dark-red hair covering half of my face. Her flowery scent filled my nostrils as I pulled in a breath and moved her hair. I stared down at her, tracking my gaze across her hand covering my chest over my heart, and down to her legs which were on either side of mine, her knee drawn up real close to my cock.

I trailed my tongue over my bottom lip and stirred when I realized I could still taste her on my lips. I wasn't sure what had woken me, but now that I wasn't asleep, all I wanted was a repeat of last night.

My hand drifted down her naked back, and

down to her ass, my whole palm covering one of her cheeks. I pressed my fingertips between her legs, and just as I was about to feel what I desperately needed, banging echoed throughout the house.

I snapped my hand back as if I'd been caught doing something I shouldn't, and Aria stirred from the impact. She lifted her head a little, but her eyes stayed closed, and when a second round of banging rang through the house, I rolled her off my chest, making sure not to wake her.

A pair of sweats hanging over the chair in the corner were the only things I could grab and yank up my legs as the banging got louder and brasher. What the actual fuck?

Pausing at the doorway, I took one last look at a sleeping Aria then darted down the stairs and to the front door. The banging didn't stop as I unlocked it, and when I pulled it open, I frowned. "Ford?"

He didn't greet me. Instead, he barged past me, down the hallway, and into the kitchen. I closed the door and followed him, wondering what the hell had happened. "What's going on?" I asked, halting just inside the door to the kitchen. "Is Dad okay?" My eyes widened. "Belle? Asher?"

"They're fine," Ford grunted, his gaze not moving off mine. "Is she here?"

I tilted my head to the side and crossed my arms over my chest. "What? Is who here?"

Ford laughed, but it wasn't at all humorous. It

was condescending, and frankly, was pissing me the hell off. "Don't gotta lie to a liar," Ford said and leaned against the counter. He was dressed in a T-shirt and jeans, but there was no mistaking the belt with his gun and badge attached to it.

He'd become part of Dad's team four years ago, and that meant part of the family too. They all loved him, but they had no idea the things he'd done for me. They didn't realize how close we'd become, but that didn't mean he could barge into my house and start this fuckin' shit.

"Leave," I ground out, my nostrils flaring and blood boiling. "Leave now before you regret coming into my house like this."

Ford raised a brow at me. "You think you can take me?" He pushed off the counter. "Go ahead. Try it, see how far you get." I stepped forward, about to let loose. "I'll lay your ass out, but you'll still be fucked."

"What?"

"You think I didn't notice?" He shook his head. "Fuck, Cade. Are you stupid?"

"You're pushing it," I warned him, feeling the control I had on my anger slipping.

"Nah." He strolled over to the other side of the kitchen casually. "That was you last night with her."

"Don't fuckin'—"

"Don't what?" he asked, his flip switching. He was good at what he did, that much was clear. He was acting like nothing affected him, but within a second he'd done a one-eighty. Calm and collected became angry and agitated. "Don't tell the truth?"

"I don't need—"

"You don't need what?" he interrupted, not letting me get a goddamn word in. "You don't need anyone finding out what you did? You don't need me to tell you that you fucked up? Huh?" He stepped toward me, his nostrils flaring. "What don't you need, Cade?"

"I've got no idea what you're talking about." My hands dropped to my sides, my shoulders slumping. There was only so much I could deny, but there was no way I'd tell him what I'd done last night. It was between Aria and me and had absolutely nothing to do with him. He had no right coming into my house and confronting me about something he knew nothing about.

He pointed at me. "Yeah, you do." He moved closer to me and blew out a breath. "Jesus, Cade. If I noticed and I've only been around you both once, do you think no one else has?"

My breath stalled in my chest at his words. We'd done our best to keep it a secret, and we were sure that was what we'd done, but...what if we hadn't? What if people *had* noticed? What if we were so inside our own bubble we didn't notice the eyes around us, watching and waiting.

Fuck.

"I could see it from a mile away," Ford continued and threw his hands up in the air. "What the hell are you thinking?"

"I'm thinking…I'm thinking…fuck."

"I've seen that look before." He let his head drop back and groaned. "That was the exact same look your dad had when it came to Lola. What the hell is it with you Easton men?"

"Don't compare me to him," I ground out and stepped forward, now only a few feet away from him. He raised a brow at me but didn't say anything else. "The difference between my dad and me is I haven't destroyed a fuckin' family. I didn't cheat on my goddamn wife with someone young enough to be my goddamn daughter!"

"No," Ford said, his voice so calm it was making me more irate. "The difference between you and your dad is he didn't break the law."

I screwed up my features, having no idea what the hell he was saying. "What?"

"Lola was nineteen. Your little girlfriend—who I'm guessing is upstairs right now—is seventeen."

"And?" I threw my hands up in the air, getting sick and tired of the way he was talking. He didn't understand. No one would understand the way I felt about Aria. Hell, I didn't fully understand it. She had me all out of sorts, and there was nothing I could do to stop it.

"She's underage, Cade."

"No." I gripped on to the counter. "State consent is seventeen."

"Yeah." Ford nodded and moved closer to me. "As long as there isn't more than a four-year age gap." He paused, his eyes drilling into mine. "There's eight years between you."

"What…" I blinked several times as the room started to tilt. My hands shook, and my knees started to give way at his words. That couldn't be right, it couldn't be…

"Statutory rape, Cade." His hand gripped my shoulder, and I didn't think he was aware he was keeping me upright. "Please tell me you didn't sleep with her."

"I…"

"Cade?" Aria's voice called from upstairs.

"Shit." Ford let go and paced back and forth. "You gotta break it off with her." Aria's footsteps echoed through the house as she came down the stairs. "I'm serious." His brows pulled down into a frown. "And you better hope she doesn't tell anyone. Shit, Cade." His voice lowered. "This isn't fuckin' good. Not at all."

"Oh," Aria's soft voice said, and goose bumps spread over my skin. I couldn't deny the effect she had on me. Part of me wanted to tell Ford to fuck off, but he was only speaking the truth. I'd crossed a line I couldn't come back from, no matter how much I tried. A line that wasn't just socially wrong, but legally too. "Sorry, I didn't realize…"

"No sweat," Ford said to her and slapped his palm on my back, his warning loud and clear. He didn't need to repeat himself because his words were still echoing around me over and over again. "I was just heading out." His boots drummed over the tiled floor, the beat an ominous warning of what could happen if I continued what we'd done last night. "I'll see you in a bit, yeah?" Ford said.

"Yeah," I croaked out, too afraid to turn around and see the both of them. Everything I'd worked toward for years was flashing and dissipating in front of my eyes. Statutory rape meant jail. It meant I'd be on the sex offender registry, which would ruin everything. I'd never be able to coach. I'd never be able to teach. It would all have been for nothing. I'd lose everything, and all because I'd given in to temptation and not resisted it.

The door slammed closed as Ford left, and the sound had me pushing away from the counter and spinning to look at Aria. Her soft features drew me in, but as soon as she saw my face, she frowned. "Cade? What's wrong?"

"I…" I couldn't get any words out. How the hell was I meant to explain it to her? There was no way I could tell her after last night it was over, not when she was standing there in one of my T-shirts looking like a fuckin' angel. "I need to head over to Dad's. Get dressed, and I'll take you home."

I didn't wait for her as I darted out of the kitchen and up the stairs. I grabbed some jeans and a T-shirt then headed into my bathroom. I could hear her milling about in my bedroom as I brushed my teeth and jumped in the shower.

I was being an asshole to her, but it was the only way to end it. I couldn't give her any false hope, but more importantly, I couldn't give myself any. If I left anything on the table, there was no way I'd be able to mark that line between us again. I was scribbling it in permanent marker to make sure it could never be erased.

By the time I was showered and dressed, Aria was sitting on the edge of the bed, her head down as she stared at the carpet. Her head snapped up at the click of the door opening, and she stood. "Cade, what's going on?"

"Not here," I told her, grabbing my wallet and keys off my dresser. I didn't say anything else to her as I walked down the stairs and right out the front door. I waited for her on the other side of the door, refusing to meet her gaze. I couldn't look at her eyes, not when I knew they'd pull me in and not let me go again.

This wasn't the plan I'd had for the morning after. I was meant to show her all over again exactly how I felt about her. I was meant to ask her to stay in bed with me all day. We were meant to—I shook my head and tamped down my thoughts. It didn't matter what the plan was. That was before…before I realized just how dangerous us being together was.

She shuffled past me, and I locked the door, then opened up the car. My jaw was tense as I pushed into the driver's side then reversed down my driveway. The car was silent as I drove to her apartment block, and I didn't turn the engine off when I pulled up outside it.

"I don't understand," Aria said, her voice hitching. "What happened between last night and—"

"I can't do this." I gripped the steering wheel harder. "I can't do this with you. I never should have done anything with you."

"What? What are you talking about? What—"

"You don't need to keep asking questions," I told her, my voice gruff as I cut her off. I needed to do this quick and easy, like ripping off a Band-Aid. "It's over. We had fun, end of story."

The air swirled in the car, the temperature dropping with each one of my words. I couldn't witness the anger on her face, but I could damn sure feel it.

"We had fun," Aria repeated. "Wow." The click of her belt rang out like a shot. "How fuckin' dare you." I could hear the emotion in her voice, but the anger was at the forefront. Good, I wanted her to be furious, it'd make this easier. "How dare you take my virginity and—"

"I didn't take it, sweetheart." I laughed and wanted to punch myself in the face. There was no easy way of doing this. It wouldn't end well. Nothing would end well. "You gave it to me freely."

"You're a dick," Aria said, but her tone was at a complete contrast with her words. "I hate you."

"Good."

"Look at me." I kept my gaze fixated on a couple of parked cars, not willing to give her my eyes. If I did, she'd see how full of shit I was. She'd see through my act within seconds, and there would be nothing I could do about it. "Look at me!" she screamed, and I closed my eyes. She'd never know how deep my heart was cracking. She'd never understand how much my soul was evaporating. She'd never know how much I loved her. She'd never hear the words coming out of my mouth. She'd never—

"You promised," she whispered, the anger making way for sadness, and I gripped my steering wheel tighter. I could barely breathe with her sitting next to me while I was doing this, but it was for the best—for her or me, I wasn't sure. "You promised it would be you and me always. Those were your words, Cade."

I didn't answer her. I couldn't answer her, because I had nothing to say. I *had* promised her that. I'd promised her I would always be there, but now I was destroying it. I was shattering it because I was scared of what would happen.

"You're a coward," she announced with a little more steel in her voice, but I could still hear the sadness ebbing away. The passenger door snapped open, and as she slammed it closed, I looked over at it, seeing her back and wishing I could get out of this fuckin' car and wrap my arms around her. I wished we could be what I wanted us to be…

But we couldn't.

I couldn't tell her what she meant to me. I couldn't do anything but watch her walk away.

———

ARIA

I tried to keep my head high as I walked across the lot and into the apartment building doors, but I couldn't stop the tears streaming down my face. The dam had broken, and it was now unstoppable. I desperately wanted to turn back and see if he was looking at me, but I wasn't willing to let him see my heartbreak. I wouldn't give him the satisfaction, not after what he'd just done.

"I didn't take it, sweetheart. You gave it to me freely."

I hiccupped a sob as his words echoed around in my head, and as soon as I was in the building, I leaned against the wall to steady myself. I was out of

his view now, and could finally let myself feel everything. He was right, he hadn't taken it, I'd given it to
him because…because I loved him. I'd let him have
a part of me I'd never given to anyone else, and he'd
shit all over it. He'd torn apart everything I thought
we were in only a few words. He'd taken a piece of
my heart without my permission, just like my
dad had.

I covered my face with my hands and tried to
catch my breath, but nothing I was doing was working. I was falling apart piece by piece, and the only
person who could put me back together wasn't here
anymore. How could he do that? How could he
shatter it all and not even look at me as he was
doing it?

"No, no, no, no," I murmured over and over
again, not quite believing what had happened. Only
an hour ago, I was curled up on top of him, his
large hands gripping me like he'd never let go.

But he had.

He'd let me go, and didn't think twice about it.

My cell vibrated in my pocket, but I didn't move
to answer it. I couldn't face speaking to anyone, not
right now. So I pulled my hands off my face and
looked through blurry eyes as I took the stairs. Each
step was harder to take than the last, but there was
only a few until I would be in the safety of my
apartment and alone.

I pushed my key in the apartment door and

dragged my feet as I entered. I wasn't aware of anything around me as I shuffled down the hallway. The door to my bedroom was in sight, relief on its way, silence and loneliness calling to me like a moth to a flame.

"Aria!"

I blinked, my body halting at the sound of Mom's voice, but I didn't turn to face her. I wasn't sure I could look at her and not break down even more than I already was. I wasn't sure I could open my mouth and say a word without self-destructing.

"Aria!" Her hand clutched my shoulder, and she spun me around. My gaze hit her bare legs and drifted over her body to the dress she wore. It wasn't her usual diner uniform but similar. Maybe she was trying on the new uniforms for her new diner.

Her mouth was moving, but all I could hear was buzzing, a static that wouldn't pause. Then she shoved her hand in my face, waving her fingers at me, and I finally saw it. The ring on her finger that could only mean one thing—

"Sal asked me to marry him!"

I blinked and blinked again, sure I'd heard her wrong. She wouldn't do that. She wouldn't say yes. She wouldn't—

"And I said yes!"

My nostrils flared, and I looked away from her, not able to bear seeing the happiness on her face. Why did she get to be happy when I was so sad?

Why did she get to start over? Why did she get to replace my dad?

My dad.

I placed my hand over my chest, feeling like I couldn't catch my breath. All the men in my life always left me, and it would only be a matter of time until Sal did the same, and I'd be left to pick up the pieces.

The paramedics strapped Dad to the gurney, but he didn't stop fighting.

"Where are they taking him, Mommy?" I clutched on to the back of Mommy's dress, staring with wide eyes as they started to wheel Daddy out of the apartment.

"It's okay, sweetheart." Mommy's hand drifted over the top of my head, and when I looked up at her, tears were streaming down her face. She was sad, just like Daddy had been the last few days. Only when Daddy got sad, Mommy worried, which made me worry.

"I'll be back, Aria!" Daddy shouted, still trying to get out of the tight straps wrapped around his body and to the bed. "They can't get you while I'm gone! Remember to cover your window at night!"

I nodded, silently promising I'd do as he said. I wasn't sure who "they" were, but Daddy was always worried about them.

· · ·

Everything was bubbling up inside me, but I had to push it down. If I let it come to the surface, it would boil over, and I wouldn't be able to stop it.

"Cong…" I cleared my throat and tried a second time. "Congratulations, Mom."

Mom grabbed my hand and pulled me down the hallway and into the living room, seemingly oblivious to what was going on with me. I went willingly, not able to get up the courage to tell her I was hurting. I couldn't voice what I was feeling, so I did as I was told and sat on the sofa.

I listened to her talk about how Sal had proposed at the new diner last night after the cookout. She told the story of a perfect moment, and all I could think about was what I had been doing last night. I'd thought I was safe. I thought I'd put my trust in someone who deserved it.

I was wrong.

I'd been stupid.

I'd let my guard slip.

I'd let him break each of my walls down, and now I was scrambling to put it all back together again.

"So? Will you?" I shook my head and widened my eyes at Mom. I had no idea what she was talking about. "So that'd make you my maid of honor, and I was thinking Belle could be my flower girl. What do you think?" I opened my mouth to reply, but she beat me to it. "Yes, that'd work well. We could get you matching dresses." She screwed up her nose. "Maybe not fully matching, but you get the idea." She clapped her hands and jumped off the sofa. "I need to call Lola!" She scrambled across the room to her cell.

I kept my gaze on her as she pressed it to her ear and started talking a mile a minute to Lola through the line. I was happy she was happy, but that didn't mean I didn't envy her. She was making a new life for herself, and I didn't think I had a place in it anymore.

"An engagement party?" Mom's brows flew high on her head. "Yes! That's a perfect idea!"

I stood, my muscles aching more than they ever had, but I wasn't sure if it was because of last night or because I was losing myself. I was lost in the wind with no branch in sight to grasp.

One last look at Mom told me she hadn't even noticed I'd moved off the sofa. She never noticed anything, but it wasn't anything new.

I shuffled down the hallway, opened my bedroom door, and shut it behind me, determined not to come back out.

Chapter Fourteen

ARIA

Monday came and went, but I didn't move from my room. I told Mom I was sick, and she didn't even come inside to see if I was telling the truth. She told me she'd get me some meds after her shift and left a couple of minutes later.

Tuesday whizzed by with my bed and comforter to keep me company.

My cell vibrated with several messages from Hope on Wednesday, but they went unanswered.

Thursday Sal knocked on my door, but I ignored him.

Then Friday came.

Friday was the best day of the week—or it had been before. Before I'd given myself over to someone who hadn't wanted me.

Mom knocked on my door. I ignored her, and seconds later, her footsteps moved away. I rolled over and pulled the covers over my head. I hadn't been expecting her to come into my room. I hadn't expected her to rip the covers off me. I hadn't expected her to demand I get up.

"I've let you have four days off school," she said, her voice firm and demanding. "It's time you push down whatever is going on and get on with things." I stared up at her, wishing some kind of emotion would bubble up. Anger at being told to push everything down. Sadness because she didn't even ask what the matter was. But there was nothing. I felt nothing.

"Now, get up." She pulled on my arm, and I let her drag me out of bed and across the hallway to the bathroom. She switched the shower on as I leaned against the sink, not willing to look in the mirror.

"I've got an important business meeting in the next town over today," she rambled on, testing the water in the shower. "Get showered and dressed, then I'll drop you off at school."

She patted my cheek twice, but I didn't look away from the small crack in one of the floor tiles. The door clicked closed behind her, and I wasn't sure how long I stood there until I pulled my clothes off and stepped under the spray. The hot water batted against my skin, trying to wash away the pain embedded into me, but it wasn't successful. Nothing I did made anything appear, I was a shell, and part of me wanted to stay that way. At least then, I wouldn't have to feel anything.

I brushed my teeth and left my hair wet as I went back into my bedroom. Black jeans and a black T-shirt were the first things my hands landed on, and I pulled them on. My boots were last, and then I grabbed my bag.

Time moved by in chunks, and then I was in the car with Mom as she pulled up in front of the school. I was late, but I didn't care.

"Sal said he tried to talk to you yesterday." I unclipped my belt and opened the passenger door. "He was trying to tell you he's bought us a new house. We're moving next weekend." I paused, waiting for the anger or happiness to break free, but…nothing. I nodded and pushed out of the car, slamming the door behind me and then walking up the steps.

I went to the office, got my late slip, and shuffled to my first class. My second class flew by, but I didn't do any of the work. I stared at the board, thinking and feeling nothing.

Lunch came, and I heard my name being called by Hope, but I ignored her, just like I had all week. But it was Jasmine's voice that finally broke my trance.

"Ugh, you're back. I'd hoped you died." My

fingers shook as I put the code into my locker lock. Her friends all laughed from behind us, but I didn't look at anything other than the chipped paint covering the metal. The lock unclipped, and I pulled on it and grasped it in my hand. "Maybe you could have killed yourself like your dad did." I took a step back from my locker. "It'd do us all a favor."

I turned, and everything slowed down as I looked at her. She was flinging things at me, and even then, I didn't feel anything. What the hell was wrong with me? The lock bit into the palm of my hand, and before I could even think about what I was doing, I flung it at her face.

The metal connected with her cheek and she squealed. Maybe I should have smiled at the sound, or even been shocked at what I'd done. But I simply stood there, waiting. Waiting for her to retaliate, because maybe if I felt the pain, it'd be better than nothing.

"You stupid bitch!" she screamed, and then gripped my hair, yanking on it. Her palm connected with my face, and then her fist followed. "I'm gonna fuckin' kill you!" I didn't move as she slammed my body against the locker and rained her fists on my face. I stayed still as she kneed me in the stomach, only feeling the loss of breath at the last second. My body bowed forward, my instincts kicking in, and then finally, *finally*, I felt something.

I lifted my head, blood trailing from my lip

down my chin, my one eye swollen from her violence, but it was what I needed. Everyone blurred around me, the only thing mattering was Jasmine as she went to hit me again.

I grabbed her wrist, stopping her momentum. "Thank you," I said, a second before I raised my fist and punched her in the temple, knowing it'd knock her out. She went down, the back of her head smacking off the solid ground.

Silence surrounded us, but I didn't look away from Jasmine and her still body. She'd given me back the feeling, but now it was evaporating again. It was disappearing before my very eyes. It didn't come back when someone grabbed my arm and demand I go to the office. I saw the back of Cade's head as he rushed into the nurse's office with Jasmine's sister, and even then, I didn't care. I didn't care about anything or anyone because it was safer that way. It was safer to feel nothing than everything.

Paramedics rushed into the office, and I rolled my eyes. I'd knocked her out, not killed her. She always was a drama queen, but at least she'd given me hope for a few minutes. Hope I wasn't completely gone. Hope that this was only a phase and not how I'd feel forever.

The office phone rang, footsteps rushing in and out, students' voices calling from the other side of the wall of windows that separated the hallway from the office. But all I did was keep my gaze glued to an anti-bullying poster attached to the wall. It was ironic. Jasmine had been throwing insults at me for years, but now I'd fought back, and I was the one waiting for the principal to call me into his office.

Justice was never served. I learned that a long time ago.

"Miss Sayer?" a deep voice called, but I didn't look away from the poster as I stood. I walked over to it, tracing the letters and wondering how many people actually believed the bullshit written on there. The teachers didn't give a crap if someone was being bullied. All they cared about was putting in their hours and then going home. "Miss Sayer," the voice repeated, this time more demanding.

I flicked my gaze over to the principal and noted the frown on his face. Of course he was frowning. He was having to actually deal with something. Just like everyone else, he loved to pretend things in this school were fine.

"Good afternoon, Mr. Smegly," I said to him, causing his nostrils to flare. I had nothing to lose, but he wasn't aware of that. He'd find out soon enough.

———

CADE

I paced out front of the school, waiting for Sal's truck to come into view. I scrubbed my hand down my face and through my hair for what felt like the thousandth time. The school was buzzing with talk, but it didn't matter what anyone else was saying. A teacher had seen what Aria had done. She'd watched her knock Jasmine out, so there was no way of getting past this.

Willow's screeching voice was still batting around in my head, threatening to press charges, and there were only two people who I could call that I knew would help. The office had tried to call Jan, but her cell had gone to voicemail. Which left Sal and—

My dad's Mustang followed Sal's truck into the lot, both of them parking right in front of the steps, not caring one bit about the fact they weren't parking spaces. They all filed out, and I was hyper-aware of Ford pushing out of Dad's car.

"What the hell is going on?" Sal asked, his face a mask of anger. His protective instincts were at full height, but so were mine. This was my fault. She was lashing out because I'd...

No, I couldn't think about that right now. I couldn't remember the way her voice sounded the last time I spoke to her.

"Aria got into a fight," I told Sal, and put my

hands on my hips. "She knocked another student out."

"Holy shit," I heard Ford whisper, and I narrowed my eyes on him. I wanted to blame him too, but the fact was he'd been looking out for me. "I didn't think she was the scrappy type."

"She's not," Dad ground out. "Where is she?"

"Principal's office." I spun around and jogged up the stairs, knowing they'd all follow me inside. "The other girl's sister is threatening charges. She's a teacher at the school." I met Dad's stare, a silent conversation happening between us. There was no way he'd let her get charged for this, or at least, I hoped.

I pulled the door to the office open and kept my gaze focused forward. The principal had told me to call Aria's parent or guardian, and he had no idea my dad would be walking through that door with Sal. They protected their family, and I was doing my best to protect mine too. Aria may think I didn't care, but that was furthest from the truth. I cared—way too much.

Aria's dark-red hair was a matted mess on one side, and it took all my strength not to go to her to make sure she was okay. Jasmine was taking up the nurse's office, which meant Aria was stuck in here.

The principal stood and frowned as all four of us filed in. "Who—"

"This is Sal," I said, waving my hand to him

and spotting the way Aria's back straightened at the sound of my voice. "He's Aria's guardian."

The principal—Mr. Smegly—held his hand out to Sal who shook it. "And these two gentlemen?"

"Special Agent Easton," Dad said, offering his hand next.

"Special Agent Ford," Ford said, shaking the principal's hand too.

"Oh," Mr. Smegly blinked and stepped back to sit in his seat. "I wasn't aware someone had called the authorities yet."

"I'm Aria's uncle," Dad said and crossed his arms over his chest. Technically he wasn't, but Mr. Smegly didn't need to know that.

I stepped back and leaned against the wall, not prepared to leave this office. I kept my gaze fixed on Aria, wishing she'd look my way, but she didn't. She didn't turn to look at anyone else in the room, keeping her gaze fixated to Mr. Smegly.

Mr. Smegly cleared his throat and steepled his hands on his desk. "As you may be aware, Miss Sayer assaulted another student."

"That right?" Sal asked, gripping on to the edge of the empty seat next to Aria. I wasn't sure whether he was talking to Aria or the principal.

"Ye-es," Mr. Smegly replied. "Aria knocked the other student out, which I'm afraid means an automatic suspension. We don't condone bullying in this—"

Aria's laugh cut him off. She laughed so hard she bent over in her seat and gripped her stomach. My eyes narrowed at the movement, and I wondered what the hell was going on. Why was she laughing when she was in trouble? Now wasn't the time or place for her to lose her shit.

"Miss Sayer!" Mr. Smegly shouted, his voice rattling around the room.

"Watch your tone, teach," Sal growled out. "You don't raise your voice at her." He pointed at Mr. Smegly. "Got it?"

"I—"

Aria lifted her head, and I stared at her as she gripped the sides of her chair and stood. "That girl has been flinging insults at me since the first day I started here." She stepped forward but kept her hand attached to her ribs. "Not once have I bitten back. I've never said a word to her, not when she stole my gym clothes, not when she called me names, but a girl can only take so much." Aria's head turned, and she looked straight at me. "I can only take so much before it becomes *too* much."

Her words broke part of me, and I knew she was trying to convey more than what had happened in the fight. She wasn't breaking apart; she'd already shattered before my very eyes.

"Jesus fuckin' Christ," Dad's voice boomed. "Has she had medical treatment?"

I shook my head, the mist around the edges of

my eyes clearing, and I finally got a proper look at her. Her one eye was swollen shut, dried blood above it, along with her cut lip. Dark purple bruises were forming on her beautiful face, and I had no doubt she had bruised ribs with the way she was holding on to them.

"I…" Mr. Smegly pulled at his collar. "Not yet. The victim has been in the nurse's office."

"Victim?" Sal growled out.

I couldn't take my eyes off Aria as Ford stepped forward. I hated how close to her he was. That was meant to be me, not him. "Lemme look at you." Aria turned her head, and his eyes roamed over her face. My hands clenched into fists as he gripped her chin. I couldn't bear watching someone else touch her.

"She needs to get checked out," Ford told Dad.

"Come're, baby girl." Dad held his hand out to her, and she didn't hesitate to take it. She trusted him. She trusted him more than she trusted me, and I only had myself to blame.

"I'm gonna sue your fuckin' school!" Sal shouted. "I'd bet my bottom dollar the other girl don't look half as bad as Aria."

"Mr.—"

"Don't you fuckin' mister me." Sal slapped his hand on the desk. "You're done. You hear me? Fuckin' done."

I stepped forward as Ford opened up the door

and followed him out, but turned back to see Dad's arm wrapped around Aria's shoulders. "Call the authorities, Mr. Smegly," Dad said. "Be sure to tell them who I am and that you kept a minor away from medical treatment."

I winced as he said minor, and my back straightened. It was just another reminder of who I was and who she was.

"Please see these people off the school grounds, Cade," Mr. Smegly told me, his whiny tone trying to sound authoritative. "You have a one-week suspension, Miss Sayer."

No one said another word as we all filed out of the office and into the hallway. The bell rang for the next class, and students started to file out of the classrooms, but they all kept to the edge of the hallway and toward the lockers as Dad, Ford, Sal, and Aria walked down the middle.

I couldn't catch what Dad was whispering to Aria, but I didn't move my gaze off the back of her head. She'd needed me, and I hadn't been there. I was never there when the people who mattered most needed me.

"She deserved it. The ginger bitch had it coming," I heard a football player say, his back to us. He wasn't aware we were here, but we'd all heard him loud and clear. My hands clenched into fists, and I growled so loud I was sure they all heard me.

Ford darted forward and slammed his face

against the locker. "What did you say, boy?" We all halted, but I didn't make a move to stop him. I'd heard what Aria had said in the office. She'd had this from Jasmine since the first day, which meant she no doubt had it from the football players too.

"Hey! Get the fuck off of me!"

"Listen good, boy," Ford growled. "You think you're a fuckin' big shot right now, but all it takes is one person to bring you down." He let go of him and the football player—Harry—spun around, his fists raised, but he stopped his momentum when he looked up at Ford. "You know what my job is?" Ford didn't wait for a reply. "I'm DEA, which means I put drug dealers behind bars. You deal drugs, fuckboy?"

"Wh-what? No, sir."

Ford tilted his head to the side, his gaze roving over him and then the other students watching. "Good." He backed away a step. "Now excuse me, my family needs medical attention." Ford brushed his hands off as if he had something on them. "You know Aria, right?" Harry's gaze flicked over to me, his eyes widening, but there was no way I was going to step in and stop him.

"Ye-es, sir."

Ford nodded and tutted. "Shame about what happened, but I heard no one saw it." Ford shrugged. "What did you hear?"

"The…the same?"

Ford grinned and slapped him on the shoulder. "Good for you, boy. I best be going now." Ford hooked his thumb over his shoulder, moved back to us, and we all started to walk out of the main doors.

"Jesus, Ford," I whispered to him.

"I only did what I knew you wanted to," he murmured back, his eyes connecting with mine. "We'll make sure she's okay."

"I'm coming with—"

"No," Ford said as Dad pushed inside of Sal's truck with Aria and Sal. "You stay here. You ain't gonna do anything good if you come with us right now." His eyes narrowed, and I knew he was only looking out for me, but that didn't mean I liked it. "I'll call you later and let you know what happens, yeah?"

I blew out a breath as Dad called out to Ford and threw him his keys. "Meet us at the hospital," Dad told him.

Ford stepped away from me, and my gaze connected with Aria. I didn't know what I was expecting as she looked at me, but it wasn't the emptiness I saw. It knocked me back a step, but as soon as I got my bearings, Sal was screeching out of the lot, taking a piece of me with him.

ARIA

I shouldn't have looked at him as we pulled out of the lot. I wasn't even sure why he was in the office with the principal, and I had no idea why it was Sal who turned up.

"Think you got some explaining to do, Ri," Sal grunted as he took the highway. We weren't heading to the diner or the apartment, that much was clear.

"She said something I didn't like," I told him, my voice bland and lifeless. I didn't want to explain to him that her bringing my dad up had made a switch in me flip.

"Yeah?" Sal said, his voice getting deeper. "What would that be?"

"I…" I closed my eyes and winced at the pain radiating in my ribs. I didn't even realize she'd gotten me in my stomach, but it had all happened so fast. "She talked about my dad."

The cab in Sal's truck went silent, and when I opened my eyes, I could barely breathe.

"Hey, hey." Uncle Brody's hand flattened on my back and rubbed up and down. "In and out. Take a breath, baby girl." I shook my head and opened my mouth, about to tell him I couldn't. I hadn't been able to take a full breath in what felt like years. "Slowly, do it with me."

I turned my head and kept my gaze connected

to his dark-brown eyes and his features so similar to Cade's. I didn't want to admit that calmed me somewhat. I wanted to deny the way Cade made me feel, how his presence in the principal's office had calmed my racing heart.

But it was the truth.

He'd destroyed everything we had, but it didn't mean I didn't need him as much as the air keeping me alive.

Sal took a turn and entered the hospital parking lot, pulling up outside the main doors. "Why didn't you tell us what was going on?" he asked, moving his head to face me, his voice sounding broken. His brown eyes met mine, and for the first time since I'd known him, I saw the pain echoed inside of them. I'd heard stories of how Sal had grown up. The rumors circulated, especially in towns like ours, but I hadn't paid them much attention.

However, I was seeing him in another light, and it made me open my mouth and tell him, "There wasn't any point."

His frown marred his brow. "Why? You know I would have stepped in and protected you."

I shrugged. "Snitches get stitches?"

His lips quirked on one side, and he shook his head. "True. Damn, Ri, I hate that she's been doing that shit with you for years."

"It is what it is, Sal." I blinked, trying to keep

the building tears at bay. "It would have only gotten worse if I'd told someone. You know that."

"Don't mean I gotta like it," he grunted out. "Far as I'm concerned, she got what she deserved." A throat cleared behind me a second before the passenger door opened. "What?" Sal asked Brody.

"Nothin'," Uncle Brody replied and extended his hand to me. "Let's get you checked out, baby girl."

I placed my hand inside his large one and let him help me out of the truck. "You coming?" I asked Sal.

"I'm gonna go get your mom and bring her back here."

My stomach dropped as another car pulled up behind us, then Ford exited. I swallowed at his presence. He'd stuck up for me to Harry, but I couldn't help blame him for what had happened that morning with Cade. Everything had been fine until he turned up.

We watched Sal pull away and then headed inside. Ford spoke to someone at the front desk, and then we were ushered into a room, not having to wait with all the other people. I had a feeling he was using his badge to get us to jump the line, but I wouldn't comment on it, not when my ribs were pulsating, and my eye was thumping to match the rhythm of my heart.

Uncle Brody waved at the hospital bed and helped me up onto it before he sat in the chair next to it. Ford took position next to the door, his gaze fixated to a spot above my head. Ten minutes went by, silence surrounding us until the chime of Uncle Brody's cell went off. He pulled it out of his pocket and murmured something down the line.

He clicked a button on his screen. "You're on speaker," he grunted.

"Aria!" Lola's voice shouted down the line.

"Lola." A smile lifted the corners of my mouth, and I groaned as the cut in my lip stung.

"Oh my god, what happened, sweetheart?" I opened my mouth to try and tell her, but she didn't give me the chance. "Brody said you got into a fight and now you're at the hospital. It was that girl, wasn't it?"

"I—"

"I knew it! I knew it was her."

"Wait," Brody intercepted. "What are you talking about, darlin'?"

"Freshmen year," Lola ground out, and I could imagine the anger on her face. "Remember when Jan was sick, and I took Aria to school for the week? I told you about that girl who pushed her against the wall."

I blinked, remembering exactly what happened. Jasmine had cornered me in the lot, but I'd forgotten my bag in Lola's car, and she'd brought it back to me. She'd heard Jasmine calling me names and witnessed her slamming me against the wall.

"It's no big deal—" I tried to say.

"Yeah, it is, baby girl," Uncle Brody ground out and stood. "Why didn't you tell us, Lola?"

"What?" Lola's voice lowered. "I did tell you, but you told me it was just high school shit."

"Fuck." Uncle Brody scrubbed his hand down his face. "We should have—"

"Guys," I held my hands up in the air. "Stop, please. It's no one's fault. I dealt with it. I doubt she'll come at me again." I blinked and stared at Uncle Brody and then at Ford, who was watching us. I didn't know what possessed me to ask him, "Right?"

His lips slowly lifted into a grin, and he pushed his hands into the pockets of his jeans. "Nah. She won't say another word to you. Especially since you knocked her out." I couldn't help my own lips quirking at his words. "Where'd you learn that anyway?"

"Where do you think?" Lola announced over the line.

"Should have known it was you," Uncle Brody said, but his tone was light now.

"What? You think I'm not gonna teach my girls how to defend themselves?" *My girls.* I was one of her girls, whether I wanted to be or not. There were times I felt so alone, but I had a family around me. A family not related by blood but who protected me like I was. "I won't have my own mistakes repeated. You know that, Brody."

"I'm sorry," I whispered, tears springing to my eyes. "I'm sorry."

"No, no, no," Lola murmured. "You don't have to be sorry for anything, sweetheart."

"Damn straight," Ford grunted. "You were defending yourself."

"But—"

The door swung open, and Uncle Brody snatched his cell off the bed and pressed it to his ear, ending the call. A man in a white lab coat entered and looked around the room.

"Of course it's you," he said to Ford.

"What? You not pleased to see me, Doc?"

The doctor grunted and closed the door behind him. "What happened here, Miss"—he looked down at the clipboard he was holding —"Sayer."

"I got into a fight."

The doctor's face didn't move an inch as he ambled toward me. "Where does it hurt?" I pointed at my ribs and then waved in front of my face. "Got it." He prodded at my face and checked my eye. "You need an X-ray on that eye to make sure your socket isn't broken." He pulled at my lip. "Your lip should heal within a week." He lifted my T-shirt up, and I realized this dude had no bedside manner at all.

"Ouch!" I gasped a breath as his fingers prodded the left side of my ribs.

"Jesus, Doc, take a little care, yeah?" Ford grunted and pushed off the wall.

The doctor raised his brow and turned his head slowly to face Ford. "Do I tell you how to shoot that gun?" He tilted his head to his belt but didn't give him the chance to answer. "No. So don't tell me how to do my job." He turned back to me. "You need an X-ray here too." He scribbled something on a piece of paper on his clipboard and pulled it off then handed it to Uncle Brody. "Follow the signs. I'll come back when I've looked at them. A nurse will come and clean your face for you."

I blinked at the doctor as he exited the room without another word, but as soon as he was gone, the door was flinging open again, and Mom was flying into the room.

"Oh my god! My baby!" She darted toward me, her hands waving in front of me, too scared to touch me. "What happened?"

"I got into a fight."

Mom's eyes narrowed. "First day back and you get into a fight? What has gotten into you lately, Aria?"

"I told you what happened, Jan," Sal said from the doorway. "It wasn't her fault."

"I know," Mom replied to him but didn't take her gaze off mine, "but it's not like you to retaliate." I could see the disappointment on her features, but more importantly, I could see the shadows in her eyes. Shadows that questioned if I was okay—not physically, but mentally. I wasn't sure what was worse: her being scared of who I was becoming, or me embracing it and not caring what anyone else thought anymore. I was lost in a sea of sorrow and pain with no one in sight to save me.

"I know it's not," I told her. "It won't happen again."

She stared at me, searching my eyes for something I knew she wouldn't find because I was shutting down in front of her. I was closing myself off to anything she could find out.

"Okay," she whispered and stepped forward, taking my hand in hers. "Has a doctor come and seen you yet?"

"Yeah," Uncle Brody answered for me, his voice gentle now. "She needs to go have some X-rays, and then a nurse is gonna come and clean her up."

"Okay," Mom said again. "Okay." She blew out a deep breath. "I suppose the silver lining is you're not at school for the next week."

"Really, Jan?" Sal asked, his voice sounding frustrated. "That all you're thinking about right now?"

"What would you like me to think about, Sal?" Mom asked, turning to face him. "I refuse to wallow in the past." I wasn't sure she knew how much her words stung. She's done an expert job at not living in the past, and I wished I knew how she managed it.

I frowned at her and regretted it as soon as my eye stung. "I don't understand…"

"We're moving next Saturday, remember? I told you this morning. At least you'll have extra time to help pack things away."

Was she really…did she…I flicked my gaze to Sal, but he was looking down at the floor now, and Uncle Brody was reading the paper the doctor had given him, but Ford shook his head. A muscle ticked in his jaw, and when his eyes met mine, I knew he wasn't happy. I'd noticed how observant he was, which was probably why he was such a good DEA agent, but it also meant he saw the things everyone else seemed to ignore.

"I can take her to the X-ray," Ford said and stepped forward. "I've been there plenty enough, so I know the way."

Uncle Brody handed him the piece of paper, and Ford extended his hand to me. "Come on, Tyson."

My shaky hand reached for his, and then his rough palm connected with mine as he helped me off the bed. The room was silent as we exited, and once we were at the X-ray waiting room, Ford said, "I know what it's like to have a mom who pretends everything is always okay." I didn't acknowledge his words as he sat in the chair beside mine. He stretched his legs out in front of him. "You gotta learn not to be like that. You keep pretending and pushing things down, you'll eventually explode."

I turned to face him and stared at the side of his face. Scruff lined his jaw, and his high cheekbones led to his hazel eyes. "I…don't know what to say to that."

"Don't need to say anything. You gotta do you, but don't think you're alone." He met my stare. "Lola and I grew up in the shittiest neighborhood. We fought for our lives every day, but that don't mean because you got the security of four walls and food in your belly that you're not fighting too." He didn't move his gaze off mine. "You got people who care about you, Tyson. People who will go to bat for you. I know you know that."

"Cade," I whispered, knowing exactly who he was talking about.

Ford clipped his head in a nod. "He'll do anything for you, even risking his freedom."

"What?" I didn't understand what he was saying. What did he mean risk his freedom?

"Ahhh, shit. He didn't tell you, did he?" Ford let his head drop back. "Jesus Christ. He told me he ended things with you—"

"Wait." I placed my hand on his arm. "What are you talking about?"

He rolled his head to the side to meet my stare. "I know about the two of you." He paused to drive his point home. "I also know he broke up with you because of what I said to him."

"What"—I licked my lips, feeling a lump form in my throat—"did you say to him?"

"I told him the facts. I told him he'd broken the law. I told him"—Ford sat up straighter—"I told him he'd committed statutory rape."

My breath stalled in my chest, and I placed my hand over my heart, sure it would evaporate if I didn't keep it locked inside. "I…"

"Look, I ain't got nothin' against you, Tyson. I think you're cool in that quiet, nerdy way. But shit, you're seventeen, and he's twenty-five. He'd be fucked if anyone found out. We're talking jail and the sex offender registry."

My breath caught in my throat as everything started to lock into place. He hadn't wanted to finish things with me. His words in his car were meant to hurt so I'd hate him, but it was all to push me away from him. He was trying to do the right thing, but it didn't mean I'd forgive him. He should have told me. I'd have understood, but he decided to take it all on his shoulders because…he didn't think I could handle it.

He didn't think I could handle it.

Was I just a delicate person on the brink of disaster to him? Is that how he saw me?

"Miss Sayer?" a voice called.

I took one last look at Ford, absorbed all of his words, and then erected my wall so high no one would ever be able to climb it again. Cade may have been protecting himself, but now it was my turn to do the same.

Chapter Fifteen

ARIA

Boxes filled with everything I'd collected in the seventeen years of my life surrounded every surface. My bed was dismantled and ready to be taken to the moving truck. My drawers were empty, my closet bare, and all that was left was the bedside table I kept my secrets in.

"Aria? You nearly finished?" Lola asked from the bathroom.

The apartment was full of people helping us move from this apartment to the new house Sal had bought. I hadn't seen it. I hadn't wanted to see it. They were starting a new life, and I wasn't sure there was any space for me in it anymore.

Things were changing, more than they ever had before, and all I wanted was something to—

I darted to my bedside table and plucked out my black case. The case I stared at for way too many hours to be healthy. It held all the secrets that kept me sane. Secrets no one could know about. No one but Cade.

Footsteps echoed closer, and I spun around, hiding the case behind my back. "Aria?" Lola asked.

"I'm finished," I told her.

She smiled at me, but it was a sad kind of smile. They all knew what had happened last week at school. My week suspension was coming to a close, and I wasn't sure how I felt about going back to school on Monday.

I'd kept myself buried away in my room for so many hours, and now it was coming to an end. I'd be somewhere new. Somewhere I hadn't grown up. The thought had my gut churning.

"I'm gonna take this out into the living room for the guys," Lola said, holding up a box of toiletries. As she walked away, I took one last look at my room. It had been my salvation when I'd needed it most. I inhaled a deep breath and shook my head. This apartment was haunted with memories, so maybe it'd be a good thing moving out of it.

I unzipped my school backpack and shoved the case inside it, not wanting anyone to stumble across it as the boxes were being moved across town, or for it to get lost. I couldn't lose the one thing I needed most in this world.

Laughter filled the apartment as I moved down the hallway, but as soon as I stepped into the living room, it all drifted away. I'd stared at the same spot for hours and hours at a time, but I'd never looked at it knowing it was the last time.

The carpet had been replaced because the bloodstains couldn't be scrubbed out of it, but that didn't mean his body wasn't still there. His ghost haunted the spot, and I swore this part of the living room was colder.

The space where his chair used to sit was empty. It had been since *that* morning. Nothing could ever replace what was once there, both Mom and I knew that, and neither of us tried to put anything there. It was a silent agreement we'd stuck to.

My body swayed forward, and I placed my clammy palm against the cool wall. I stared at it in shock, remembering the blood splattered over it.

"Aria?" Mom frowned as I stepped back. "Honey, what's going on?" I shook my head, my mouth opening and closing like a fish, but no words would come out. "Is it because we're moving?"

I turned to look at her, my feet unsteady. "Dad," I managed to croak out.

She heaved a breath, almost as if she was fed up with hearing his name. "Stop thinking about it." Her voice was different now, farther away, but closer all at the same time. I stared at her, really stared at her, and realized how much she'd changed. The sadness that used to surround her was replaced with happiness, and the slump of her shoulders wasn't there any longer.

"I—"

"It was nine years ago," Mom ground out, her tone telling me she didn't want to talk about it. She never wanted to talk about it, and that was part of the problem. She never wanted to speak to me about what I'd seen. She never wanted to acknowledge what I saw on a day-to-day basis. She never wanted to admit what had happened.

"Nine years, ten months, and sixteen days," I croaked out, backing up another step and causing my back to hit the wall. My skin crawled at being pressed against it, but it was stopping me from falling.

"Aria—"

I held my hand in the air to stop her. "It doesn't matter how much time passes." I sidestepped across the wall, trying to get away from her—trying to get away from everything. "It doesn't matter how much you want to pretend it didn't happen." I tapped the side of my head with two of my fingers. "My memories are burned inside my brain. Nothing I do ever gets them out."

"Honey, please, I don't want to talk—"

"You never do!" I slapped my hand against the wall, the vibrations shooting up my arm and making me grit my teeth. "You never want to talk about it! You never want to talk about anything!"

"Aria, that's enough," Sal's deep voice gritted out, and I looked past Mom to see him standing in the living room. He'd tried to help me as much as he could after the fight at school, but none of that mattered in this moment. Nothing fuckin' mattered anymore. "Don't talk to your mom like that."

I laughed, but the movement made tears fall from my eyes. Tears of pain no one cared about. "You think you can try and be my dad now, Sal?" I raised a brow. "You wanna treat me how he did, huh?"

"Aria, don't," Mom pleaded, and any other time, I'd have accepted her request and walked away, but something was urging me on. Something was telling me to air all the pain built up inside of me.

"What?" I flung my gaze to hers and pushed off the wall. My feet carried me to the entrance of the kitchen, and I held my arms up. "Have you not told him what he used to do to me?" Mom was silent, her eyes shined with unshed tears. "I was a kid. A fuckin' kid." I ground my teeth together. "But you were never there!"

"Aria," Lola called from across the room, but I couldn't see her. I couldn't see anything but the blood staining the floor and walls.

"My first memory of my dad is him carrying me

to the roof and making me balance on the edge." A sob broke free, but the dam had been opened, and there was nothing I could do to stop it. "He told me I'd die if I didn't stay there for one hundred and seventy-four minutes. He stood there and counted them down."

I closed my eyes, remembering the way the edge of the roof dug into the soles of my feet. I could still feel the rough surface of them, and all it made me want is to scrub it off my skin.

"Then there was the time with his gun." I tried to swallow past the lump in my throat, but it was useless. "He made me take turns holding it to his head. What was it they called it? Russian roulette?" I opened my eyes, my gaze landing on Mom, who had tears streaming down her face. "I didn't know it wasn't loaded." I tried to heave in a breath, but nothing would get through the blockage in my throat the memories were causing. "Where were you then, Mom?" My voice was small, but when she didn't answer me, I shouted, "Where the hell were you?"

"Stop, Aria." Someone touched my arm, and I darted away from them, feeling like my skin was burning from their touch. "Please, sweetheart," Lola's voice broke through. "Please stop crying."

"Don't you see?" I asked Mom. "It doesn't matter how much time passes by. It doesn't matter how much better your life becomes because I will never be the same. I'll always have his memory etched into my mind, refusing to let go."

"Baby," a deep voice whispered from beside me, right before his hand landed on my wrist. His fingers connected with my skin, and for half a second, I forgot the amount of pain he'd caused. I forgot how he threw me away. I forgot that Cade walked out on me, just like *he* had.

"Don't touch me," I warned him, my voice low. "Don't you ever touch me again."

"Please," he begged. "Please stop."

"Stop what?" I screamed. "Stop telling the truth? Stop bleeding my pain out in front of you? You want me to hide it again, Cade? Huh?" I backed away until my back hit the counter. "That's all anyone ever wants." I looked down at my feet, my gaze tracking the edge of my boots and up the laces. "Everyone just wants me to pretend," I whispered.

I pounded my fist on my chest and gritted my teeth from the shock of pain it sent through my ribs, but it didn't matter. I was trying to push it back down, but it was impossible for it all to fit inside. I'd opened Pandora's box, and I wasn't sure how to put the lid back on.

"We don't," Lola said from somewhere beside me. I could still feel Cade close by, his aura warming me and making me feel safe—safe from everyone and everything. "We don't want you to pretend, sweetheart."

"Honey," Mom's voice croaked, and I whipped my head up. Tears were still streaming down her face, and it was only then I noticed everyone else standing and watching. Uncle Brody was near the door, blocking the entrance to all his guys, but they were seeing it clearly. They were witnessing my meltdown. They were seeing the crazy running through my veins.

"It's okay," I told her, slamming the door to my emotions shut and welding it closed. "It's okay." I wasn't sure whether I was trying to convince her or me, but the more I said it, the more I started to believe it.

I pushed off the counter, my legs shaky as I took a step forward. My heart raced, my pulse thrumming, but I tried to control it all. I tried to put a lid on it and act how they all expected. "Let's go to the new house."

"Okay, honey," Mom whispered right away, as if she was afraid I'd change my mind.

"Are you serious?" Cade asked, his gruff voice cutting through everything else.

"Cade," Lola warned, but I wasn't sure what she was warning him about. It didn't matter either way. I'd pushed it all down, and now I was Aria again. Or at least a version of her they wanted me to be. I'd flipped the switch *just like that.*

"No." Cade's footsteps came closer, and I felt him behind me rather than saw him. "You can't push this down, Aria." His hand drifted to my arm, and his fingers wrapped around the soft skin. "Don't do this to please her. Feel it, baby. Let it all out. You can't bury it."

I turned my head and stared at him over my shoulder. "I can." I dropped my voice to a whisper. "I'm full of secrets I'll never tell."

"I don't give a shit." A muscle in his jaw ticked, and he shuffled on the spot. "You can't keep doing this."

"Doing what?" I asked, raising my brow. "I'm not doing anything."

I didn't wait for him to say another thing as I yanked my arm out of his grip and walked across the living room, leaving the ghost of my dad behind as I told myself I could start fresh. I repeated it over and over again, sure the more I said it, the more it would come true. I was starting over. Creating a new life, cleaning my slate of all the bad memories.

Starting fresh.

———

ARIA

The new house was only a five-minute walk to Uncle Brody and Lola's. It meant I could walk to school and not have to rely on Mom or Sal giving me rides, and it would give me more independence. I should have been happy about it, but I felt... strangely calm. Calm about everything going on around me. Calm about the people coming in and out of the new house.

My heart beat a steady, slow rhythm. My eyes soaked in every corner of the house, most importantly, my new bedroom. There weren't remnants of aluminum foil stuck to the edges of the window, and the inside of my closet doors weren't covered in the stuff. It was brand new, a fresh start.

I'd slept on the mattress on the floor last night, but Sal had just finished putting the bed together, and now my furniture was being placed inside the room. It was twice the size of my old one, and I hated it. I hated the space. I hated the light that shone through the big windows. I hated how I didn't feel safe here. The walls were white and lifeless, much like me. The wood floor was dark oak and felt cold, much like my skin. It wasn't somewhere I wanted to be, but I didn't have a choice.

"Aria?" a voice I knew so well called, but I couldn't even bring myself to smile as Belle ran into my new bedroom. She gasped, her eyes widening. "Wow. This is huge!"

I nodded and stared around the room. "It is."

"Are you going to decorate it?" she asked as she ran to my bed and bounced on it. She yanked the bow out of her hair, screwed her nose up at it, then threw it on the floor. I didn't know how many times Lola was going to keep trying to get her to be girly.

"I don't know," I told her, sitting on the edge of the bed next to her. "I hate the white. It's so—"

"Cold," Belle interrupted. "You should paint it black."

I raised my brows at her words. "Black?"

She nodded and steepled her palms together then pressed the tips under her chin as she assessed the room. "Yeah. That wall could be black. You could make it into a chalkboard wall!"

I tilted my head to the side and stared at the wall. It wasn't a bad idea if I were honest. It would also give me something to do and keep my mind occupied off the fact tomorrow was my first day back at school. "Wanna help me?" I asked her.

"Yes!" She jumped off the bed and grabbed my hand then dragged me from the room and down the stairs. Belle was a girl on a mission. "Ford!" She bypassed Mom and Lola in the hallway and headed right for Uncle Brody and Ford. "We need a ride," she told him, planting her hands on her hips as she stared up at him.

"That right, Baby Belle?" Ford asked and crouched down in front of her. His lips spread into a smile I'd not seen on his face before, one specially reserved just for her.

"Yep." She nodded several times. "We need to go to the DY store."

"DY?"

"DIY," I interrupted. "She means DIY."

"Okay." Ford dragged the word out. "And what are we going there for?"

"Paint, duh." Belle threw her hands up in the air and rolled her eyes. "Come on, let's go." She grasped my hand again and pulled me across the room. "Oh, I need to get some money from Uncle Sal." She let my hand go and ran back up the stairs, but still, I couldn't seem to smile up at her. She always managed to break through everything and have me feeling like me, but today it wasn't working. She had a sixth sense on how to cheer people up. I just wished I could allow myself to feel it.

"Aria?" Mom called. "Where are you going?"

"To the store," I told her and ambled over to her and Lola. "Belle wants to help me paint my room."

Mom bit down on her bottom lip, her gaze flicking to Lola and then back to me. "I think we need to talk first."

"Talk?" I frowned and took a step back. Mom never wanted to talk, not unless it was about something that didn't really matter.

"Yeah." Her breath was audible as she let it out. "About yesterday."

Silence stretched between us, neither of us willing to take the conversation any further. I'd exploded in the apartment yesterday, but I'd pushed it all down because that was what she'd wanted. I'd adhered to her request, so she couldn't change the rules of the game now.

"You need to talk it out with your mom," Lola said, her voice soothing, but it did nothing for me. All it made me do was shutter everything down even more than it already was.

"No." I shook my head and took another step back. "I don't need to talk."

"You do," Mom insisted. "You have too much anger—"

"Anger?" I laughed, but it was only to cover up the sadness bubbling up inside me. "I haven't got any anger."

"You do." Mom stepped forward, but my instinct was to back away even more. "What you said yesterday wasn't fair. You blame me for—"

I shook my head. "I don't." Lies. All lies. I did blame her. I blamed her more than she'd ever know. And this was just another reason why. She didn't think it was fair I'd aired her dirty laundry in front of everyone, but if she really cared about me and not what other people thought of her, we'd not be in this situation.

"Aria," Mom huffed out.

"What?" I shrugged and raised my hands in surrender. "I'm doing what my mom does." I backed away a final step to stand in the doorway.

"I'm gonna sweep it under the rug and forget all about it."

"I don't do that."

"Sure, okay, Mom." My shoulders slumped. "I can't deal with you right now. I'm...I'm done." Two words. All it took was two words to snap everything out of me. My vision blurred, my world turning from color to black and white. I was done with everything.

I was done trying to be perfect.

I was done pretending.

I was done trying to be the person they all wanted me to be.

I was going to embrace who I felt like I was inside—a black hole with no end in sight.

Chapter Sixteen

CADE

I leaned against my classroom door, brought my coffee cup to my lips, and gazed around at the students milling about the hallway. They were all heading to their lockers before lunch, but it wasn't them I was really looking at. I was searching for a certain dark-red-haired girl.

I knew it was her first day back, but I hadn't seen her since I helped move them out of the apartment. I hadn't gazed at her face since she exposed herself in a way I never knew was possible. Remembering the pain-filled words made my heart ache, and I rubbed my chest with my palm to try to alleviate it.

I'd never wanted to fight so hard for someone in my entire life, but it wasn't my place. I couldn't stick up for her the way I wanted to. I couldn't help her. I couldn't do anything but be her teacher and coach, and that was what hurt the most.

"Hey, Cade," Willow's voice called, and I turned my head to see her pushing her way through the students in the hallway. The smile on her face was megawatt as she flashed it at me, and I did my best to return it.

"Hey," I murmured, pushing up off the doorframe.

"How's your day—" Willow cut herself off, a gasp leaving her mouth. "What the hell?"

I frowned and tried to see what she was staring at, and that was when I saw her. She clutched her books against her chest, her head down, her hair covering most of her face. The bruises from last week had disappeared, her swollen eye now back to normal, but that didn't mean she was pain-free.

"I can't believe they've let her back in this school." Willow crossed her arms over her chest as Aria stopped at her locker and opened it up. "She should have been permanently removed after what she did to my sister."

"And your sister?" I asked, not looking at Willow. I couldn't take my gaze off Aria as she pushed her books inside and flinched when someone barged past her. I had no doubt she was getting verbal abuse today. I knew how high school worked, and there was no way she could get away from what she'd done to the head cheerleader.

"She's doing better now—"

"No." I finally snapped my gaze off Aria and whipped my head around to face Willow. "I mean, shouldn't Jasmine have gotten the same punishment as Aria?"

Willow's brows came low over her eyes, her cheeks starting to turn pink at my words. "What?"

"Jasmine isn't innocent."

"What?" Willow's nostrils flared, and her hands fell beside her waist. "She knocked my sister out, Cade. What more do you need?"

"And your sister didn't fight back?" I raised my brows for effect. "Your sister didn't split Aria's lip and blacken her eye?"

"Yes, but she was defending—"

I shook my head and took a step back. "If you believe that, really believe it, then you're just as bad as she is."

"Cade!" Willow shouted, gaining the attention of the students milling around us. Aria walked by us but didn't make a move to look at me. Today was Monday, which meant track practice, but I had no idea if she was going to turn up or not. "You can't say that."

"Miss Simmons." I closed my classroom door and locked it. "It was nice talking to you." I walked past her and sauntered down the hallway toward my office. I wouldn't stand there while she acted like Jasmine wasn't to blame. I had no doubt Aria shouldn't have done what she did, I wasn't excusing that at all, but there was only so much of one thing someone could take until they snapped.

I got changed out of my shirt and pants and into my sweats then headed for the track. I needed to run off some of the tension my body was holding on to.

By the time I'd done ten laps around the track, took a shower, and was dressed in fresh sweats, the end-of-school bell rang. I headed out onto the field and waited for Reagan and Aria. Part of me wasn't expecting her to turn up, not after everything that happened, so when she walked out of the building side by side with Reagan, I tried to mask my surprise.

"One jog around the track to warm up, girls."

Neither of them spoke to me as they took off around the track. I stood motionless as they jogged, my stomach dipping with every stride Aria took. She was going too fast for a warm-up, but I didn't say anything about it. I was just glad she was here.

I tasked Reagan with improving her one track time and then turned to Aria. "We need to work on your long-distance and endurance today." She was staring down at the grass beneath her sneakers as I spoke to her. "Three laps, I'll be timing you."

She lined up at the starting line and then took

off. Each lap she ran faster than the previous, and when she'd finished, she'd set a new personal best. Sweat was rolling down her face, her cheeks bright red from the exertion.

"Take a breather and then go again," I told her, but she didn't take a break. She started up the next three laps and went at it harder than before. She was running away, she just didn't realize she'd never be able to outrun herself. It was an impossible task I was all too familiar with.

Reagan improved her time with each lap, and when she hit the time I'd set for her as a goal, Aria was on her last lap. "You can head in and get changed, Reagan. Good practice today."

"Thanks, Coach." She spun around and jogged across the field and into the building. She'd made it through the door when Aria came to a stop ten feet in front of me.

"What are you doing, Aria?" She kept her gaze locked on the ground, and I itched to step forward and grab her chin so she'd give me her eyes. My fingers twitched at the thought, but I managed to keep my feet planted to the grass. "Aria?"

"Am I done, Coach?" her soft voice asked.

I dipped my head back and stared at the clear blue sky. I had no idea what to do or say to her. I was afraid I'd say too much or too little. There was no winning the game we'd played, only losing.

"Yeah, Aria. You're done for today."

She nodded three times in quick succession but didn't move. My gut churned at the thought of her possibly looking at me or saying more than the bare minimum, but it soon disappeared when she turned around and walked across the field.

I didn't move from my spot when she entered the building. I stayed where I was for another fifteen minutes, hoping, by the time I went inside, she'd be gone because I wasn't sure what I would do if we were alone again. I'd spill it all and say fuck it.

And I couldn't risk everything just to touch her one more time.

———

ARIA

I didn't know ninety percent of the people filling up the diner, but apparently, they knew me. Their faces all blurred together as they said hi to me.

The whole place had been transformed into a party space and closed to the general public. I wasn't sure why Mom and Sal decided to have an engagement party on a Wednesday evening. Maybe it was because of their schedules, or maybe Mom just didn't want to have to sit opposite me at a family dinner without a buffer.

Either way, I sat in the corner toward the back of the diner in a booth, watching everyone talk, laugh, and have a good time. Drinks were handed out, music was played, and a dance floor was created, but I didn't move from my position.

The above-the-knee dress Mom had bought me still hung on the back of my bedroom door. She didn't realize I couldn't wear it because of my scars. She simply thought I was resisting her. If only she knew the real reason.

Belle's sweaty face came into view, her mouth moving, but I wasn't hearing anything she said. All I could hear was the buzzing in my ears, and the sound of my heart beating faster and faster. There were too many people. Too many eyes staring at me. Too many whispers between people I didn't know.

I jumped as something clanged around the room, and when my gaze landed on Sal, I realized he'd tapped a knife against a glass to get everyone's attention. "I'm not good at talkin' in public," he grunted, and everyone laughed. They thought he was joking, but the people who really knew him knew he was being honest. "I just wanted to thank Jan for coming into my life and saying yes to marryin' me." He cleared his throat and pulled at the collar of his shirt. "That's all."

Mom laid her hand on his shoulder and stared up at him. "Oh, Sal." She chuckled. "A man of few words, my husband-to-be is." The happiness emanating from her was palpable. She turned to face the crowd, her gaze batting over them all, finally landing on me. I wasn't sure what she was trying to silently tell me, but I kept my stare locked on hers. "We also wanted to announce the date of our wedding."

My breath caught in my throat. How had they set a date already?

"Grown-ups are so boring," Belle whispered to me, but I didn't look down at her. I kept all of my attention on Mom and Sal as she looked back at him and then out at the crowd.

"Christmas is just around the corner," Mom started, "so we've decided to have a February wedding."

My heart stalled, my pulse slowing down so much I was sure I would pass out. She knew what that month meant, she knew the agony and torment associated with it, and yet she chose it anyway. What was the rush? Why did they feel the need to get married so soon?

I stood, nearly toppling the drinks on the table. No one looked my way as they all cheered and spoke about when invites would go out. The air around me buzzed as I stumbled to the side and into the back of one of the booths.

"Aria?" Belle's small voice called, but I ignored her as my fingers curled around the leather, the only thing keeping me planted to the universe I'd found myself in. I tried to slow my breathing down, but nothing was working. I was trapped, and I couldn't see a way out.

I finally looked up and stared at the door. I mentally counted the number of steps it would take, and then took one at a time. By the time I pulled the door open, the world was tilting, and my breaths were pants I couldn't gain control over. I knew my reaction to them setting a date wasn't normal—I knew that. But it didn't make an ounce of difference. My body had taken over, and there was no fighting to get it back.

My back scraped against the brick wall outside the diner, and I let myself drop to the ground. My palms dug into the gravel surface, the small stones biting into my skin and reminding me I was still here.

The sounds of the party were muted, but I couldn't stand to listen to them. I looked over at the windows, seeing everyone having fun, and knew I couldn't be here anymore. I couldn't sit and watch them all smile and laugh, not when I was falling apart piece by piece.

I spotted Belle talking to Ford and pointing out of the window, and when his gaze met mine, I stood. My stomach churned as I let my feet take me away from here. I let them dictate where I would go.

The music got lower as I reached the edge of the lot, but I didn't turn back when my name was called. I couldn't face anyone. I wasn't sure how long I walked for, and I wasn't sure how many miles I'd gone, but when I stopped and saw the sign for the cemetery, I realized my heart had taken me to the root of the problem.

If it weren't for the man buried in those grounds, I wouldn't be this way. I wouldn't have the memories that haunted me. My hands clenched into fists as I pushed through the gates and toward his headstone. The words etched into the surface were lies. Lies to make him look better.

Loving husband and father.

It was all a lie. A lie I'd kept hidden which had destroyed me in the process. "I hate you," I whispered, staring down at him. "I hate you," I repeated, louder this time. I backed away a step and let my head drop back, then shouted, "I hate you!"

I didn't know what I was expecting. Maybe to feel some relief. Maybe to feel different. But it didn't change anything. He was still ruining my life even when he wasn't breathing, and I didn't know what to do to change it. I had no idea how to fix what I'd become, and it was all his fault.

I took one last look at his name, burned the memory into my mind, and promised myself I'd never come back here.

Chapter Seventeen

ARIA

My Converse slapped against the concrete sidewalk as I walked into the parking lot of the school, but I didn't take in any of the faces or words slung my way. I was blocking them all out and doing my best to survive.

Survive.

Just for one more day.

I just had to get through the next few hours and make it back to my bedroom where I was safe from everything. Safe from the world. Safe from…everyone.

I jogged up the stairs and headed for my locker, intent on going to my first class. The hours dragged by, each one taking what felt like forever. Lunch came and went without Hope again. I hadn't spoken to her for weeks which was easier to do because of the holidays. Thanksgiving and Christmas had gone by uneventfully, at least, to everyone else. I was too afraid to talk to anyone, especially Hope, because I was sure she'd see through everything and figure out what was happening to me.

I didn't need her help. I didn't need anyone's help.

The bell rang out for the second-to-last class of the day. Only a few more hours and then I could lock myself away for the night inside the empty house. Students barged past me in the hall, but I was used to it now. Since I'd knocked Jasmine out, nothing much had changed, apart from her locker no longer being next to mine.

Goose bumps spread along my skin, my hair standing on end, and I looked around, trying to figure out what had caused it. I stumbled when Cade's dark-blue eyes connected with mine, but it wasn't them that had me standing still in the middle of the hallway. It was Miss Simmons' hand on his chest that had the wall crumbling down around me.

He didn't move her hand off him. He let her touch him in the same way I had.

Sometimes, all it took was one thing to knock you over the edge completely and have you falling to your death. They said you're meant to get back up when something knocks you down, but what if you're punished with blow after blow? What if each one pummels you farther into the ground until you're part of it, never able to separate yourself?

I closed my eyes, sure I was seeing things, but when I opened them back up, she was still touching him, and he was still staring at me. I didn't know what to do or how to react, so I spun around and headed for the bathroom.

My breaths heaved out of me as I halted in the middle of the room. I turned toward the sinks with small mirrors attached to the walls above them, and I blinked. Stared. I saw…nothing. There was nothing behind my eyes that were surrounded in dark circles, and my lips sat in a straight line on my face, a face that was paler than usual.

The Aria everyone thought they knew was gone, and in her place was a shell. A shell that only wanted one thing. Something I'd itched to do all week but had stopped myself, but I couldn't now. I couldn't stop my feet as they moved me toward the stalls. I couldn't stop my hands as they locked the door behind me and opened up my bag. I'd put my black case in there when we moved to the new house, and I hadn't taken it back out. I always kept it close now, just in case.

I sat down on the closed lid of the seat and stared at the door, not moving an inch. The bell rang, signaling everyone must be in their classes, but still, I didn't move. I stayed right where I was. This was always something I did at home. I may have craved and itched to do it at school, but I always managed to wait it out. Not today, though. Today I was reaching into my bag and pulling out my small case.

I kept my gaze focused on the writing on the back of the door as I stood. My body worked on automatic and yanked my jeans down, exposing my legs. My ass hit the cool seat of the toilet, and then I spun sideways, using the side of the cubicle to prop my right leg up.

My fingertips ran over the scars, the bumpy, straight lines calming me somewhat. Sometimes it was all I needed, but today was different. I needed to feel the scratch of the blade as it pressed against my skin. I needed to wince at the sharpness, and then finally exhale as the wet blood ran over my skin and dipped between the scars.

I opened my case, the zip so loud it made my ears hurt. I was doing this, here and now, and there was nothing that would stop me.

My collection of blades sat in their own little elastic holders, and I plucked out the freshest one. I needed something that would give me quick relief. Something that would make me stop feeling the way I did right then.

I balanced the case on my other leg and placed my thumb and middle finger against my thigh, cordoning off the area I was going to cut. It was lower down than I'd have liked, only an inch above my knee, but it was the only place I could go to. It was in the back of my mind that I'd soon have to find a new place, but right then, this would do.

I inhaled a deep breath and pressed the blade against my skin without any pressure. My ritual allowed me to keep calm. A ritual I'd perfected over the years. I counted to seven and pressed a little harder. By the time I made it to ten, the blade was piercing my flesh. The sharp metal dragged over my skin, but it wasn't a small cut this time, I kept going, only stopping when I finally was able to exhale.

My head dropped back and leaned against the other side of the cubicle, and for the first time today, I felt like I could finally catch my breath.

The euphoria was instantaneous.

The sharpness of the cut made me wince.

The blood flowed down my leg and made my eyes flutter.

Then it was gone.

In an instant, everything I'd felt disappeared, and I realized what I'd done and where I'd done it.

My body came alive, my brain whirring as I pulled my cell out and looked at the time. I only had ten minutes until my next class, and in that time, I needed to patch up my cut. I looked down at it and groaned. I'd gone deeper and longer than I meant to, but it was nothing a wad of tissues and some medical tape couldn't cover up until I got home.

I wrapped the blade in some tissue and placed it on top of my case as I swung my legs down. I stared at the drop of blood flowing down my calf, fascinated with how quickly it made it to my ankle.

I sighed as I pressed my hand against the cut, relishing in the burn of it. I may have gone deeper than I should have, but at least with a squeeze of my legs, I could feel the burn I so desperately needed.

———

CADE

The students for my last class of the day filed in as I stood beside my desk. They all took their seats, but I didn't move, knowing there was someone missing.

I waited an extra beat for her to show, but when the second bell rang out, I closed the classroom door and huffed out a breath. Maybe she'd decided not to come to my class after what she'd seen in the hallway.

Willow had cornered me for the third day in a row, and I couldn't get away. I shouldn't have let her touch me, but with my gaze focused on Aria, I couldn't see or feel anything but her anyway. Willow didn't matter. No one mattered, not like Aria.

I turned around, not really taking anything in, and then the door creaked open. My gaze flicked over to it, seeing Aria standing in the doorway. Her eyes were focused ahead of her, but it didn't seem like she was looking at anything in particular.

Part of me wanted to lecture her on being late, but when I opened my mouth, nothing came out. She blinked several times, but nothing seemed to clear the way her eyes appeared—empty and life-less. My stomach dropped, and my hands started to shake. She'd buried herself down so deep she couldn't find a way out.

She shuffled over to her desk and sat in the chair, her bag still attached to her shoulder as she stared down at the wooden surface of her desk.

"Pop quiz time," I announced with a clap of my hands, but even that didn't shock her into looking at me. She was in her own head, more so than I'd ever seen before. The class groaned, but it didn't matter how loud they were, it wouldn't get them out of it. I passed the sheets to the first person in each row and sat behind my desk. "You have until the end of class," I said, logging in to my laptop to get some lesson plans done for the upcoming week.

The chatter in the room quieted, and it wasn't until thirty minutes later, I finally looked back up, my gaze immediately landing on Aria. She wasn't staring at her hands anymore. Instead, she was looking down at her lap and squirming on her seat. Her eyes fluttered closed, her lips parted, and I could almost hear the sigh escape her.

What the hell was she doing?

The clock told me there were only a few minutes left of class, and from the noise now starting to surround us, everyone had finished their work. I didn't stray my gaze from Aria, though. Not to close my laptop, and not even when I stood.

"Hand your papers up front as you leave," I told the class a second before the end-of-school bell rang out.

They all shuffled to the front of the class and out the door, but Aria had yet to move. It was like she hadn't even heard me. I took a step forward, my dress shoes clacking against the floor. I hated when I had to wear a shirt and tie to work, but I didn't have a choice when I wasn't teaching PE or after-school sports.

"Aria?" I moved closer to her, now only two desks away. She didn't look up, concentrating on her hands. I frowned, hating seeing her like this, but I had no idea what to do.

My gaze roved over her, and I halted when I spotted a red stain on her inner thigh, a couple of inches above her knee. Part of it looked dried, part fresh. But it wasn't just any stain…

It was blood.

Had she cut herself at school? Were things really that bad?

"What did you do?" I asked, my voice deeper than I meant for it to be. I hated when she did this to herself, but there was nothing I could do about it, not now I'd destroyed everything between us. I'd had a choice between her and me, and I'd chosen me. I'd chosen myself over the girl who meant everything.

Her light-brown eyes met mine, but there was nothing behind them. No anger, no sadness…nothing.

"Aria?" I crouched down in front of her and placed one hand on her desk. Her finger twitched with my nearness, but it was the only indication she even saw me. "Baby? What did you do?"

"I…" Her voice was raw, almost as if she'd been screaming at the top of her lungs for hours. "I…"

A lump formed in my throat, and I tried to swallow past it, but I couldn't. I couldn't sit here and watch her fall apart and not pick up every piece to put her back together again.

"Why?" I asked, my own voice betraying me. "Why have you done this?"

"Because…" A tear fell from her eye, but she didn't move to swipe it away. It tracked down her cheek and dripped over her chin and onto her chest. "Because I need to feel again."

I couldn't resist touching her when another tear fell. My hand reached out to the side of her face, and I ran my thumb over her cheek, the pads of my fingers extending into her red hair. "What do you need to feel?" I asked, almost afraid of her answer.

She stared into my eyes, tears flowing out of

them like raindrops dripping down a windowpane. I wanted to stop the way she was feeling, I wanted to take it all away.

Her tongue swiped along her bottom lip. "Anything." She hiccupped a sob. "I just want to feel anything."

"Baby." I pressed my forehead to hers, trying to absorb some of her pain, but it was an impossible task. "I've got you, Aria. I'll always have you."

Her throat bobbed on a swallow. "I'm scared."

"I know, baby." My voice so rough, I didn't even recognize it. "But I'm here."

She opened her eyes, the light-brown orbs pulling me in more and more. She was hooking me in, not intent on letting me go, but I wanted to stay right here, just the two of us, in this bubble where nothing and no one could hurt her.

"I can't do it anymore," she whispered, so low I had a feeling she was scared to say it out loud. "I can't do any of it anymore."

I gripped her hand on the table. "I'm here," I told her. "I'm here now."

"Help me," she pleaded, and it was those two words that had a tear slipping down my own cheek. "Help me forget all about it."

I'd do anything to make her feel better. Anything at all. "I will," I promised as I pulled in a deep breath. "I'll make it all go away." I pressed my lips to hers tentatively, scared I'd push too hard, but when she kissed me back, I knew I couldn't live without this—without her. I'd made a mistake walking away from her. I should have chosen her. It should never have been a doubt in my mind.

My arms wrapped around her waist and I pulled her closer, kissing her softly and promising I'd never leave again, no matter what it meant.

"Cade?" a new voice asked, and all of my thoughts dissipated in an instant. My eyes flung open, and I yanked my lips away from Aria as my heart raced so fast I was sure it would leap out of my chest.

"Cade?" Willow's voice repeated. "What…what are you doing?"

Acknowledgments

This story became so much more than I ever thought it would. When I started Cade and Aria's book, I never imagined it would become what it is today. The journey has been epic and emotional.

My first thank you needs to go to Paige. You're the most awesomest Alpha Reader and PA. Thank you for loving my stories as much as I do, and generally just being you!

My second thank you needs to go to my husband and daughters. This book became such a huge part of my life, and I can't thank you enough for putting up with my weird ways.

I'd liked to say a huge thank you to my BETAs readers: Nikki & Yvonne. You ladies are amazeballs and I couldn't do this without your continued support!

To my bestie, Dan. Thank you for always being there for me, no matter what. You're the besets friend a girl could ask for! Love you long time!

To my ARC team. You ladies are simply amazing and I love for each and every one of your messages! Thank you for taking the time to ready my stories, I appreciate so much.

To the bloggers who help share EVERY-THING. I love you so much, and I can't put into words how grateful I am! You are a special bunch of people who continue to put a smile on my face.

Linda, thank you soooo much for everything you do. You're always there no matter what, and I'm not sure what I'd do without you! You push me when I need to be pushed, and tell me to slow down when I need to stop. You save my ass more times than I can count, and I love you!

To my editor, Jen, thank you so much for every-thing you do. You make me a better writer with each book, and you're so much more than an editor. You've become my friend, and I wouldn't be without you!

My proofreader, Judy. Thank you for putting up with me! I continue to use commas in the wrong places and you continue to correct me. Never leave me, because I'd be lost without you!

To all the authors in the community. You continue to support me and I can't thank you enough for that. I love our little slice of heaven, and wouldn't want to be anywhere else!

Lastly, I want to say thank you, to you. Thank you for taking a chance on this book. Thank you for reading. And thank you for being awesome!

Also by Abigail Davies

MAC Security Series (Alpha Security/Military)

Book 1: Fractured Lies

Book 2: Exposed

Book 2.5: Flying Free (Standalone Spin-off)

Book 3: The Distance Between Us

Book 4: ReBoot

Book 5: Catching Teardrops

Six Book Boxset

———

The Easton Family

Fallen Duet (Forbidden Angst)

Book 1: Free Fall

Book 2: Down Fall

———

Confessions Series (Romantic Comedies)

Book 1: Confessions Of A Klutz

Book 2: Confessions Of A Chatterbox

Book 3: Confessions Of A Fratgirl

A. A. DAVIES (Darker, alter ego)

Verboten (Extreme Taboo. Inferno World Novella)

Broken Tracks Series,
(co-authored with Danielle Dickson)

Book 1: Etching Our Way

Book 2: Fighting Our Way

Destroyed Series,
(co-authored with L. Grubb)

Destroying the Game

Destroying the Soul

About the Author

Abigail Davies grew up with a passion for words, storytelling, maths, and anything pink. Dreaming up characters—quite literally—and talking to them out loud is a daily occurrence for her. She finds it fascinating how a whole world can be built with words alone, and how everyone reads and interprets a story differently.

Now following her dreams of writing, Abigail has found the passion that she always knew was there. When she's not writing: she's a mother to two daughters who she encourages to use their imagination as she believes that it's a magical thing, or getting lost in a good book.

If she's doing neither of those things, you can be sure she's surfing the web buying new makeup, clothes, or binge watching another show as she becomes one with her sofa.

Connect with Abigail

Reader group—Abi's Aces
Newsletter

www.abigaildaviesauthor.com

facebook.com/abigaildaviesauthor

twitter.com/abigailadavies

instagram.com/abigaildaviesauthor

goodreads.com/abigaildavies

bookbub.com/authors/abigail-davies

amazon.com/author/abigaildavies

pinterest.com/abigaildaviesauthor

Printed in Great Britain
by Amazon

29768237R10175